Emma looked at Ku

He's so han... so much about me ... the kind of guy I could really spend my life with. And I'm thinking about going to Africa next year? *And then a voice inside her said,* If he really cares for you, he'll be here when you get back.

"Emma, I want to support your dreams," Kurt said earnestly. "One of the reasons I fell for you is that you have them!"

"So, then—?"

"So, it's not so simple anymore," Kurt said. "Maybe in romantic novels two people stay together even if they're separated for a year or two, but that's not necessarily how it is in real life!"

"But if we really love each other . . ." Emma let the rest of her sentence dangle in the air. Kurt was right. She could tell herself that he would be here when she got back, but there weren't any guarantees.

Am I really willing to risk that?

The SUNSET ISLAND series
by Cherie Bennett

Sunset Island
Sunset Kiss
Sunset Dreams
Sunset Farewell
Sunset Reunion
Sunset Secrets
Sunset Heat
Sunset Promises
Sunset Scandal
Sunset Whispers
Sunset Paradise
Sunset Surf
Sunset on the Road
Sunset Embrace

Also created by Cherie Bennett

Sunset After Dark
Sunset After Midnight
Sunset After Hours

Sunset Embrace

CHERIE BENNETT

Sunset™ Island

SPLASH™

A BERKLEY / SPLASH BOOK

SUNSET EMBRACE is an original publication of
The Berkley Publishing Group.
This work has never appeared before in book form.

SUNSET EMBRACE

A Berkley Book / published by arrangement with
General Licensing Company, Inc.

PRINTING HISTORY
Berkley edition / August 1993

A GLC BOOK

ISBN: 0-425-13840-2

BERKLEY®
Berkley Books are published by The Berkley Publishing Group,
200 Madison Avenue, New York, New York 10016.
"BERKLEY" and the "B" design
are trademarks belonging to Berkley Publishing Corporation.

PRINTED IN THE UNITED STATES OF AMERICA

10 9 8 7 6 5 4 3 2 1

For Jeff. You're everything.

ONE

"That is the biggest lasagna I've ever seen," Emma Cresswell exclaimed to the rest of the table of four as a dapper Italian waiter set her plate down in front of her. She looked down at her white miniskirt and pristine white eyelet-lace sweater and hoped she wouldn't get any tomato sauce on them. *Ah, but the Ice Princess never spills!* she reminded herself, employing the nickname that had been teasingly given to her by her best friends.

"Too bad Sam's not here," Carrie Alden quipped. "She'd have it as an appetizer!"

At that, Emma and her boyfriend, Kurt

Ackerman, and Carrie and her boyfriend, Billy Sampson, all broke into laughter.

"I've never seen a girl eat as much as Sam Bridges," Kurt marveled.

"I've never seen any living creature eat as much as she does," Billy added with a grin.

"And stay so thin!" Carrie added fervently, casting a rueful eye at her own curvy body.

Carrie is so hard on herself, Emma thought. *She looks terrific—not everyone is going to be five-feet-ten and rail-thin like Sam. I know for a fact that Sam wishes she had some of Carrie's curves!*

"You ready for the rest?" the waiter asked. They nodded, and he set down steaming plates of pasta with clam sauce, cannelloni, veal parmigiana, creamed spinach, and garlic bread.

"Welcome to the Sportsmen's Restaurant," the waiter said when all the food was on the table. "You won't go hungry. That's what we always say." He sauntered off to take care of another table.

"Yum!" Carrie exclaimed, taking a forkful of cannelloni. "Too bad Sam couldn't get tonight off," she added. "This is her kind of place."

"Yeah, but I don't think she'd be too into a slide lecture about some living fossil in Mozambique," Kurt said, rolling his eyes. "It was all Emma could do to convince me to come with her!"

Emma playfully kicked Kurt under the table. *Actually,* she thought to herself, *they're all really good sports to go to this lecture with me after dinner. I have the greatest friends.*

Emma—who was raised in an extremely wealthy, upper-crust Boston family—sometimes couldn't believe that she was actually spending her second straight summer working as an au pair on Sunset Island, a famous resort island off the coast of Maine. And she was even more disbelieving that she had Kurt Ackerman as her boyfriend. Kurt was a really incredible guy who had grown up on the poor side of Sunset Island and was now working his way through college.

Not someone that mother approves of. Not at all. His parents don't even know any Rockefellers! Well, too bad for you, Mother, Emma thought smugly.

"Hey," Billy said, gesturing with his fork, "maybe we can drop Emma off at the university for her lecture and we can all go see *Revenge of the Goober Monster* at the Maine Mall Cinema. Whoops!" A stray strand of mozzarella cheese fell off Billy's fork into his lap.

"Sorry," Carrie said, grinning as she reached over to take a bite of Billy's veal parmigiana, "we're all going to suffer through it."

Emma smiled at her friend. Carrie and Billy had the greatest relationship. She was so happy for them. Carrie was girl-next-door cute, really smart (she was a student at Yale), and a wonderful friend. And Billy was such an incredible guy. As the lead singer of Flirting with Danger (Emma and Sam were two of the three backup singers for the band, and Carrie had filled in briefly as the third when the band was on tour), girls were always falling all over him. But he was in love with Carrie.

I wish Kurt and I got along that well, Emma mused as she watched Billy playfully tickle Carrie in the ribs. Emma loved Kurt, but lately it seemed that all they did was fight. *I bet Sam wishes she and Pres got along that well, too,* she thought.

Sam was seeing the Flirts' bass player, Presley Travis. Their relationship had been bumpy, but things seemed to be getting better between them.

Better for me and Kurt, too, Emma thought hopefully, reaching over to caress Kurt's hand.

"Why are you so interested in this speech tonight, anyway, Emma?" Billy asked her. "Come on, isn't a slice-and-dice movie more your idea of fun?" he wheedled.

"Yuck," Emma commented.

Kurt picked up his bread knife and moved toward her, then stabbed it into a piece of garlic bread on the table. "Killed it!" he yelled triumphantly.

"C'mon you guys," Carrie said. "Quit ragging on Emma. You know she wants to go to Africa with the Peace Corps."

"Hey, in the words of your friend and mine, Samantha Bridges," Billy quoted, " 'you cannot use a credit card in the jungle.' "

"Oh, well, in that case forget the whole thing," Emma replied jokingly. She was used to her friends getting on her case about her family's money.

Not so long ago I would have been really

hurt, but now I can actually laugh about it, Emma realized. *Pretty good progress!*

"Listen, Em. I think you should start to concentrate on your singing," Billy said nonchalantly.

"Why?" Emma asked, concerned that she'd been missing notes during band practice or something.

"Because it looks like we're going into the studio soon," Billy said.

"Studio, as in recording studio?" Emma asked with surprise.

"Yeah," Billy said, grinning broadly. "Ain't that a kicker?"

"All right!" Kurt said, taking a forkful of lasagna. "How'd you pull that off?" Kurt was particularly interested in the band's progress since he'd been their road manager during a recent tour where they opened for rock star Johnny Angel.

"A combination of things," Billy replied with a shrug. "Mostly we borrowed money from everyone we know."

He didn't borrow money from everyone, Emma thought. *He never asked* me. *Why? I could have lent it to them easily. In fact, I could pay for the whole thing.*

"Billy—" Emma began, leaning across

the table to look at him intently.

"Emma, I know what you're gonna say," Billy interrupted. "And no way are we borrowing money from one of our backup singers to cut a new demo. No-no-never-never-uh-uh-uh," he chanted playfully.

"Why is it better to go to people who aren't in the band than to come to me?" Emma asked.

Billy grabbed a piece of garlic bread from the basket. "Because money is power," Billy said simply. "It would not be cool to give you that kind of power over the band," he explained.

"But I would never look at it that way!" Emma protested.

"I know," Billy said matter-of-factly. "But I would."

"Well, isn't it risky to put yourself into so many people's debt?" Emma asked, still feeling hurt that Billy and Pres hadn't come to her. "What if it doesn't turn out well? It just makes so much more sense to—"

"It's going to turn out great and I said no way, Emma," Billy repeated emphatically. "That's not the way I do things. Period, end of discussion."

"Okay," Emma said quietly, trying to accept Billy's position gracefully. She looked at the gold and diamond Cartier watch on her slender wrist. "If we don't get going, we'll miss the lecture."

"What a shame!" Kurt said with a laugh. "I really, really, really wanted to see *Revenge of the Goober Monster*, too. . . ."

"Well, it's going to be revenge of the Emma monster if I miss this lecture," Emma said, looking around for the waiter so they could get their check.

"Whew, scary thought," Kurt told his friends. "Emma on the warpath is much scarier than any horror movie!"

Emma elbowed Kurt playfully in the ribs, and finally caught the waiter's eye.

The lights came up in the main auditorium of the department of anthropology at the University of Maine. Dr. Alain Chanderot, the world-famous French specialist on evolution, was just finishing his two-hour combination slide show and lecture.

Emma had been so engrossed that she hadn't even looked at her friends since the lecture began. *Hmmmm. Billy's rubbing sleep from his eyes, so he took a nap. So is Kurt. Carrie looks like she's been lobotomized. I guess they hated it.*

"So, in conclusion," Dr. Chanderot said in his heavy French accent, "while the discovery of the australopithecus by Leakey completely revolutionized our concept of the evolution of the species, the more recent discovery of the simian's cousin near Mozambique is in many ways even more important."

The audience of about seventy-five people applauded.

"Say what?" Billy Sampson whispered to Emma.

"Sssh!" Emma said, stifling a laugh.

A tweed-jacketed professor went to the front of the lectern. "Dr. Chanderot will now answer questions."

Emma tried to listen as the French naturalist handled a couple of very technical questions with apparent ease, but she barely knew what he was talking about. Finally, she raised her own hand, cautiously.

"Yes?" Dr. Chanderot said, pointing to Emma. "The mademoiselle in the back."

Emma screwed up her courage.

I'm such a know-nothing on this stuff, I hope I don't make a total idiot out of myself, she thought. *How can I get him to take me seriously?*

Then Emma had an idea.

"Docteur Chanderot, j'ai une demande plus de practique que de theorie," Emma started out.

She saw the professor's face register the flawless French she'd learned at boarding school in Switzerland. She had caught his attention, even though all she was saying was that she had a practical, as opposed to a theoretical, question. Emma saw that even Carrie, Billy, and Kurt were listening now that she was speaking.

"Oui, mademoiselle?" Dr. Chanderot asked, seeming to respect Emma's French.

Emma switched back to English, out of consideration for the other people in the room. "If you were a student, and you wanted to get involved in research like the kind that you do, what would you advise?"

Dr. Chanderot smiled. "You have made an excellent start," he said. "Speak French, because much of your work will be done in French-speaking Africa. Learn Portuguese, for Mozambique and Angola. Where do you currently go to school?"

"Goucher College in Maryland," Emma said.

"I advise you to try a different university, one with a large research program," Dr. Chanderot said. "I myself teach at the University of Lyons, in France. That would be an excellent place for you to study. Or join your Peace Corps. That prepares you for life in the bush."

The Peace Corps! There it is again! That's what made me want to come to this lecture in the first place! Emma thought. *Of course, all I do is think about it. And thinking about it doesn't get me any closer to going to Africa.*

The question and answer period finished up and people started filing out of the auditorium. Some were gathered around the lecturer. Emma would have liked to join them, but there was only so much she could put her friends through.

"You ready to go?" Kurt asked, stifling a yawn.

"Sure," Emma said, filing out into the aisle.

She walked out of the building lost in thought. *I'm a baby-sitter in Maine during the summer, and a college student at a bor-*

ing, overpriced, snooty college the rest of the time. That's what I am. And I haven't really done anything to change my life except talk a lot of pointless talk.

Well, maybe it's time to finally do something about it.

"You're seriously thinking about going to Africa?" Carrie asked Emma as the four friends sat around in a nearby coffee shop after the lecture.

"Yes," Emma said emphatically. "You heard what Professor Chanderot said." She didn't look over at Kurt. She knew that the idea of her going to Africa made him miserable.

Emma remembered back to before she and Kurt had become a couple, when she'd confessed to him her secret desire to join the Peace Corps. *He was so supportive of me then,* Emma remembered wistfully. *But now he's so afraid he'll lose me if I go, that he isn't really supportive at all. . . .*

"But I thought that your plan was to finish college first," Kurt said in a low voice.

Emma took a sip of her tea. "I hate Goucher College, frankly," she told him.

"So transfer to the University of Maine

with me," he said with a hopeful smile.

Emma smiled back at him with love. "I just can't think of any really good reason to put off going," she said earnestly.

"Try a college degree," Kurt said a little sharply, clearly wounded that *he* wasn't a good enough reason to put off going.

"Well, I could go and then come back and finish school," Emma pointed out.

"Look, Africa will still be there after you graduate," Kurt said. "After *we* graduate," he added meaningfully.

Emma looked at Kurt thoughtfully. *Does he mean he'd want to go to Africa with me?* she wondered. *And would I even want him to?*

"Listen, I'm only thinking out loud," Emma said with a shrug, backing off a little. "I've had the application form forever and I still haven't even filled it out."

"Good," Billy said. "I'm a selfish guy—I don't want to break in a new backup singer."

"And I want to be able to visit you without having to get a visa," Carrie added playfully.

Kurt reached over and put his hand over hers. The look of love in his eyes told her everything she needed to know about his feelings.

There are so many reasons not *to join the Peace Corps,* Emma thought.

But as the conversation continued around her, all she could think about was that application form, waiting for her in her top dresser drawer.

Emma walked into the Hewitts' house just before midnight. Kurt had dropped Carrie and Billy off at the Play Café for a late-night game of pool, then he'd taken Emma home to the family she lived with and worked for.

"Don't go traipsing off to the other side of the world without me," Kurt had said when he'd kissed Emma good night. "I hear the primates over there are wild and kinky."

"Very funny," she'd murmured, burrowing into his warm embrace. She'd tried to finish the evening with a light tone, but she knew only too well how serious Kurt really was.

Emma found a carefully written note waiting for her on the kitchen counter.

Emma,

Your mother called. She and Awstin

Pain are in New York. Here is the number. 212-555-2800. It is a hotel, sweet 2717. She says call her and Awstin no matter how late you come in. I will see you tomorrow and so will Wills and Katie.

Ethan

Emma smiled, even though the idea of a midnight phone call with her mother was not her idea of a good time. She loved Ethan Hewitt's misspelling of "suite," and of her mother's boyfriend's name—Austin Payne.

It's Austin Payne himself I loathe, she thought. *He gives new meaning to the words "effete artist." And the fact that he's young enough to be my brother doesn't help things, either.*

Well, no sense postponing my fate. Mother dearest is always up late at night. Emma picked up the phone in the kitchen and dialed.

"Sherry Netherland Hotel," a bright voice answered.

Of course, Emma thought. *The hotel where all the show-business people stay.*

"Suite 2717, please," Emma said. The

phone rang twice, and then Emma's mother answered.

"Hello! Austin stop that!" Katerina Cresswell—who insisted that everyone call her Kat—said, giggling girlishly into the phone.

"Hello, Mother," Emma said politely.

"Oh, hi, Emma!" Kat responded. "Really, darling, why does it always sound like you've just eaten an unripe persimmon? Honestly, Emma, loosen up some!"

She sounds a little drunk, Emma thought to herself.

"Fine, Mother," Emma said tightly. "I'll try."

"Good," Kat said. "I called because Austin and I have exciting news."

He's decided to become a human cannonball in the circus, Emma prayed.

"What, Mother?"

"He has been selected for a very important show on Fifty-seventh Street! At Sidney Janis!" Kat sang out the name of the famous New York art gallery.

"Well, Mother, that's just . . . swell," Emma said. *Swell? Did I say swell?*

"We were thinking that you might want to make plans to come to the opening,

Emma dear. It's in two months," Kat said gaily.

"I don't think so, Mother," Emma said.

Time to change the subject. What can I ask her about? Okay—Austin.

"How are you and Austin getting along? Have you set a date yet?" Emma asked.

Kat laughed again—it sounded a little forced to Emma. "Oh, he's being his usual artistic difficult self," Kat trilled. "But he'll decide soon."

"Good, Mother," Emma said. "I've got to get to bed now. I have work tomorrow."

"Honestly, Emma," Kat said, "I still don't see why you don't quit that silly job and come with me—"

"Bye, Mother." Emma hung up the phone.

A wave of depression filled her. *It doesn't take much to ruin a perfectly good evening,* Emma thought. *A phone call from my mother where all we talk about is her. She didn't even ask how I was.*

Emma quietly climbed the stairs to her room and got undressed for bed. Then she pulled the application form for the Peace Corps from her dresser drawer.

And she began filling it out.

TWO

"So the thing is, Emma," Jane Hewitt said, "Jeff and I have decided that Ethan and Wills need to be able to handle themselves in the wilderness."

It was the next morning, and Emma had just finished clearing up the breakfast dishes. Jeff and Jane, her employers, were sitting with her at the breakfast table. They'd waited until after breakfast, then shooed the kids (twelve-year-old Ethan, eight-year-old Wills, and four-year-old Katie) into the family room to play Nintendo while they talked with Emma.

"The wilderness," Emma echoed politely, sipping her tea.

"That's right," Jeff continued. "They lead a really soft life."

Emma nodded. "You're right," she agreed solemly. "I say we ship them off to Marine boot camp."

"Can you imagine that?" Jane asked with a laugh.

"Seriously, though," Jeff said. "When I was a kid I was in the Boy Scouts, and we'd go hiking, canoeing, whatever."

"I've tried to get Ethan and Wills interested in joining but they just look at me like I grew two heads," Jane said, sipping her coffee. "I can't even sell them on the idea of sleep-away camp—I loved hiking wilderness trails when I was at camp . . ." Jane reminisced.

"I guess it's just not something that appeals to them," Emma said simply.

After being forced to go to ballroom dance class and perfect-manners class and everything else my mother insisted was crucial for me when I was a kid, I'm not exactly sympathetic to forcing kids to do things they have no interest in, Emma thought.

"I know normally we don't like to push the boys into anything they don't really want to do," Jeff said, as if he were reading

Emma's mind, "but Jane and I talked this over last night, and—"

"And we have a feeling they'll really like it if they just try it," Jane said earnestly.

"Builds character," Jeff said in a portentous voice, mocking his own seriousness.

"Anyway, we're going to give it a try," Jane said. "Then if everyone hates it, we'll drop the whole thing."

"Okay," Emma said slowly. She could hear Ethan and Wills in the family room, playing Nintendo, and giving little shouts of glee whenever they achieved a particularly good result. *Wills and Ethan are really good kids, but Wills hates bugs and lately Ethan doesn't go anywhere without his Walkman.*

"So," Jane said, "what we've decided is, we're going camping tomorrow. Actually, mountain climbing. To Mount Washington."

"Wow," Emma breathed softly. *Mount Washington is the biggest mountain in New England. People go skiing there in June, so much snow falls in the winter. I think my dad went there to ski when he was in college. . . .*

"Doesn't that sound terrific?" Jane asked,

interrupting Emma's reverie.

"I think it's great, Jane," Emma said, mustering as much enthusiasm as she could for what she thought could easily turn out to be a nightmare. "I'll take really good care of Katie while you're gone and—"

"Oh, that's not the plan at all," Jane explained easily. "You're coming with us."

"I'm what?" Emma asked dully.

"Coming on the mountain-climbing trip," Jane said. "Jeff will stay here with Katie."

I'm going with them? Okay, I'm going with them. Help!

"Have you ever done any hiking?" Jeff asked her.

"Uh, gee, a little . . ." Emma hedged.

Sure I've hiked, Emma thought ruefully. *I've hiked all over the big department stores in Paris, and once I went for a walk in the Alps. This does not qualify me as the Great White Hunter!*

"Great!" Jane said. "I've got an extra pair of boots—good thing we're the same size—and all the camping stuff we'll need is in the basement. I'm going shopping for the boys later. We'll leave at eight A.M. tomorrow. It'll be fun!"

It'll be a riot, Emma thought grimly. *Usually Jane and Jeff have really great ideas about things to do with their kids, but I have a feeling that this is not going to be one of them.*

"Camping? Hiking? Mountain climbing?" Kurt asked Emma with a laugh. The two of them sat together on a makeshift swing under a tattered awning in Kurt's backyard.

"I'm praying that this rain keeps up," Emma said, watching a few drops of rain work their way through a hole in the awning. "Maybe our trip will be rained out."

"No dice, sweetie," Kurt said, kissing Emma's cheek. "Tomorrow's forecast: clear and sunny. You're outta here! Bon voyage!"

"Gee, thanks," Emma said sarcastically. "You just think the idea of me roughing it in the great wilderness is hilarious."

"That's true," Kurt agreed. "Bring me back photographic proof."

A clap of thunder rumbled, followed by a streak of lightning across the sky.

"Maybe we'd better go in," Emma suggested. "At least the rain gave you the afternoon off today."

Kurt worked two jobs—one of which was teaching swimming at the country club. Normally he still had to work even if it rained—he just used the indoor pool. But today the indoor pool was having some sort of structural repair work done on it.

"Want some hot chocolate?" Kurt suggested when he saw Emma shiver. They walked in the back door and Kurt opened a cupboard, looking for a pot.

"Sure," Emma said. "Just remind me that I have to leave by three to pick up Wills and his friend.

Kurt put some milk on the stove, then took Emma in his arms. "Maybe I will, and maybe I won't," he teased her. He pressed his lips against hers and kissed her, first lightly, then passionately.

"Wow," Emma said breathlessly. "You sure do know how to make me forget."

"Good," Kurt murmured, pulling her close again.

"Wait," Emma said, backing away. "I want to ask you something."

Kurt looked at her. "Why do I have a feeling this is serious."

"Well, it's not that serious," Emma assured him. "It's about the Peace Corps."

"Oh, that," Kurt said flatly. He went to the stove to make the hot chocolate.

"You remember when I first told you that I wanted to join?" Emma asked, sitting at the kitchen table.

"Last summer when we first went out," Kurt remembered.

"Right," Emma said. "Do you remember how you were so encouraging then, how you told me to follow my dreams?"

"That was before," Kurt said, bringing two cups of hot chocolate over to the table.

"Before what?" Emma asked, even though she already knew the answer.

"Before I was in love with you," Kurt said simply. "And before you were in love with me."

"But why should love make us turn our backs on our dreams?" Emma asked plaintively.

"It's not that simple, Emma," Kurt said in a low voice, blowing on his steaming hot chocolate.

"You have dreams, too," Emma reminded him. "You told me once that you were thinking about politics."

"I still am," Kurt admitted. "The nice

thing about politics is that you can do it right here in Maine, instead of in the African jungle."

Emma looked at Kurt closely. *He's so handsome, and smart, he cares so much about me—he's the kind of guy I could really spend my life with. And I'm thinking about going to Africa next year?* And then a voice inside her said, *If he really cares for you, he'll be here when you get back.*

"Emma, I want to support your dreams," Kurt said earnestly. "Hell, one of the reasons I fell for you is that you have them!"

"So, then—?"

"So, it's not so simple anymore," Kurt said. "Maybe in romantic novels two people stay together even if they're separated for a year or two by a few continents, but that's not necessarily how it is in real life!"

"But if we really love each other . . ." Emma let the rest of her sentence dangle in the air. He was right. She could tell herself that Kurt would be here when she got back from Africa, but there weren't any guarantees.

Am I really willing to risk that? she wondered. She took a sip of her hot chocolate.

"So, if you were going to go into politics you'd have to go to law school, right?" Emma asked, eager to change the subject.

Kurt nodded. "Probably at Orono. Then, I'd like to come right back here to Sunset Island. I think Jade Meader's already planning for me to run COPE."

Emma knew that COPE stood for Citizens of Positive Ethics, a political-action organization on Sunset Island that was trying to preserve the island from overdevelopment, as well as improving the living conditions of a small and very impoverished part of the community.

"That's great, Kurt!" Emma said warmly. She'd done some volunteer work for COPE at various times during the summer. "You never told me that before."

"Well, it's just a thought," Kurt said. "But I do know that I want to make my home here on the island. I guess that doesn't surprise you."

"No, it doesn't," Emma said with a smile. Kurt's love for this island that had always been his home was very apparent.

"You think you might have a future here?" Kurt asked in a low voice.

This was a subject that never failed to make Emma nervous. Kurt wanted them to discuss their future together—marriage even—and Emma just didn't feel ready.

"Right now I'm more concerned about having to go mountain climbing tomorrow!" Emma said lightly, draining the last of her hot chocolate.

Kurt stared at her a minute, then he let the heavy subject drop.

"Okey dokey, rich girl, come with me," Kurt teased, getting up from the table. "It's time for a crash course from Wilderness Guide Ackerman—Everything You Ever Wanted to Know About Hiking and Camping but Were Afraid to Ask! And if you're even *thinking* about joining the Peace Corps someday, this stuff just might come in handy."

"Excuse me, girlfriend," Sam said to Emma later that day. "Did I hear you say *camping*? You've got to be kidding."

"Nope," Emma said, "I could not be more serious."

It was early evening, and Emma, Sam, and Carrie had all met at their favorite bench at the end of the main pier to watch the sunset.

"Maybe Jane thinks you're not working

hard enough, Boston Baroness," Sam wisecracked, "so this trip is some kind of punishment!"

"Not working hard enough? Are you kidding?" Emma exclaimed. "Listen to today—Katie had her play group in the morning, then from three to five I took Wills and another kid to the movies, then I made dinner for all three Hewitt kids because Jane and Jeff were out shopping, and then—"

"Okay, I'm convinced," Sam said. "It's not punishment. But it should be!"

"I think it sounds like fun," Carrie said with a shrug.

"Well, thank you so much, Nature Girl," Emma said with a laugh. "How about if I suggest that you go in my place?"

"Would I get to take Billy?" Carrie asked with a lascivious grin.

"Somehow I doubt it," Emma replied. She looked out at the sun as it set over the endless sea. "That is so beautiful," she breathed softly. "I wonder what a sunset looks like in Africa. . . ."

"Just like this sunset," Sam said, "only a wild beast is gnawing on you while you contemplate it."

"Not all of Africa is wild," Emma pointed out.

"Yeah, but it is where they send Peace Corps volunteers," Carrie said.

"True," Emma agreed. She watched the fireball of the sun dip below the horizon. "I filled out my application form last night."

"You *what*?" Sam asked.

"Filled out the application form," Emma repeated. "As much as I could, anyway. They need my college records, all kinds of things—"

"You're really serious about this!" Carrie marveled.

"I guess I'm finally figuring out that talk is cheap," Emma said lightly. "I've been talking about it forever. . . ."

"Well, if it's what you really want to do, I think it's great," Carrie said firmly.

"What about Kurt?" Sam asked.

"That's the tough part," Emma admitted. "He doesn't want me to go—"

"Can you blame him?" Sam queried.

"No," Emma replied, "and yes. The no part is I understand he's afraid we'll lose what we have together, and the yes part is that if he really loves me, he should support what I want to do."

"Love is not supposed to hold you back," Carrie said firmly.

"I agree," Emma said softly, scratching a mosquito bite on her leg. "So why does it feel to me like it so often does?"

"Sam's doing *what*?" Emma asked Wills Hewitt later that night. Wills was sitting on the edge of his bed in his Boston Red Sox-imprint pajamas.

"Going with us mountain climbing," Wills repeated. "Tomorrow. To Mount Washington."

"You're kidding," Emma said.

"Unh-uh," Wills said, crawling into bed. "Mom thought that you'd want company so she called Mr. Jacobs and now Sam and Allie are coming with us."

"Oh, come on," Emma chided, "that can't be true. Samantha Bridges? My friend Sam?"

"It was supposed to be a surprise," Wills said, shrugging contritely. "I guess I blew it."

"I'm finding this really hard to believe," Emma said, not knowing whether she should laugh or cry. "Sam actually agreed to this?"

"I guess," Wills said. "Can you leave the Batman on?" he muttered, burrowing under his covers. Wills had recently unearthed his old Batman night-light and had been wanting it on at night. It embarrassed him, since he considered himself too mature for something so babyish. And it didn't help that Ethan had been teasing him about it at every opportunity.

"You got it," Emma assured him, plugging in the night-light. "Sleep tight!" She kissed his cheek (which he actually allowed, as long as Ethan wasn't around to tease him) and walked to the door.

"'Night, Emma, see you in the morning. Early!"

That's right, Emma thought, quietly closing Wills's door. *We're leaving at eight o'clock. That means breakfast is probably going to be at seven. That means Jane is going to wake me at six-thirty. Fabulous.*

Then Emma realized that Sam was going to have to wake up at the same hour. *And we all know how much Sam hates getting up early!* Emma laughed to herself. She went to her room and picked up the phone and dialed Sam's number.

"Jacobs residence," Sam answered. "Sam Bridges speaking."

"Hi, Sam," Emma said casually. "What's new?"

"Emma!" Sam cried. "This is all your fault!"

"My fault?" Emma said innocently.

"Yes!" Sam insisted. "I've got to have someone to blame! I mean, *me? Mountain climbing?* The only mountain I want to climb is Pres!"

"Life's tough, huh?" Emma laughed richly.

"Oh, you!" Sam sputtered. "You're actually enjoying this!"

"Guilty," Emma agreed.

"Ha," Sam barked. "It's just that misery loves company."

Emma smiled and balanced the phone between her shoulder and her ear. "The grapevine says that Allie Jacobs is coming along, too," Emma ventured.

"The grapevine's right," Sam replied. "Dan wanted the girls to split up for once, so Becky got off the hook. You can imagine how thrilled Allie is. First she tried faking being violently ill, but her father didn't believe that one. So then he bribed her with the purchase of the outfit of her choice at the Cheap Boutique if she'll go."

"That's not a very healthy ploy," Emma observed.

"Yeah, tell me about it," Sam said. "But Dan Jacobs is not what I would call a father from the 'how to' book."

"He tries, I guess," Emma remarked.

"Well, right now what he's trying is my patience," Sam wailed. "This was not in my job description!"

"Maybe it'll be fun," Emma ventured.

"Right, and maybe Saddam Hussein will be picked as the next pope," Sam said dri- ly.

"What the hell am I supposed to pack?" Emma heard Allie Jacobs yelling in the background.

"What do I look like, Girl Guide of the Mountains?" Sam yelled back.

"Gee, I guess you're busy getting ready," Emma said innocently. "I'll let you go."

"You're going to pay for this, Emma Cresswell," Sam said darkly.

"How's that?" Emma asked, stifling a laugh.

"I'm going to tell Allie that you offered to lend her all your clothes," Sam said smug- ly. "She'll be on your doorstep within the hour."

"See you tomorrow, nature lover!" Emma said gaily, and hung up the phone.

Camping. And mountain climbing. With Sam, Emma thought ruefully. *Well, if I live through it, this should be a once-in-a-lifetime experience!*

THREE

"Emma!" Ethan Hewitt's voice sang out up the stairs. "Telephone's for you! Don't forget we're leaving in fifteen minutes!"

"Thanks, Ethan," Emma shouted as she finished lacing up the hiking boots Jane Hewitt had lent her. "I'll get it."

Who could be calling me at this hour? she thought to herself. *No way it's Sam—she's too busy getting ready—or rubbing sleep out of her eyes. Kurt's definitely asleep. Maybe Carrie? But why would she be calling me so early? To wish me luck? Okay, that's it, I'm sure it's her.*

"Carrie, there's no need for you to call to wish me luck," Emma said into the phone.

"Just because we're going mountain—"

A male voice chuckled at the other end of the phone.

"Emma?" the voice said. "I'm not Carrie, or at least I wasn't the last time I looked. It's your father."

Emma froze.

My father? Last time I saw my father was on Paradise Island, when I won that trip there and took Sam and Carrie with me. Dad showed up there after breaking up with that young girlfriend. We did decide that we were going to make an effort to try to get to know each other better, but I haven't heard from him since.

Emma composed herself. "Hi, Dad," she said, as brightly as she could manage. "I just didn't expect that you'd be calling me this early."

Her father laughed, a little uncomfortably. "I thought maybe you just didn't expect that I'd be calling at all."

"Well, now that you mention it. . . ."

"It's okay," Emma's father said. "I'm not very good about staying in touch, am I?"

"No, you're not," Emma agreed.

"I'd like to remedy that," Emma's dad said warmly. "I've got good news."

"You're marrying a fourteen-year-old and you want to fly her to the island so I can give my blessing?" Emma asked sarcastically.

There was silence on the other end of the phone. "You don't make this easy, Emma," Mr. Cresswell finally said.

Emma felt a quick pang of guilt. She really didn't dislike her father—not the way she disliked her mother, anyway. And there had been moments when she'd felt as if maybe, just maybe, they could have a closer and better relationship. But something always came up with him to spoil it—some business deal, some other obligation—and the moment always seemed to pass.

"Sorry," Emma apologized. *Try not to feel so defensive,* she counseled herself. *At least listen to what he has to say.*

"What I was going to tell you is that the Inches's have invited me to use their place this weekend," her father said.

The Inches's? Who are they? Emma wondered. Then she vaguely remembered that when her mother and father were still married, they were friends with a couple who had a summer house near Rhode Island.

"Gee, great, Dad," Emma said, puzzled. "So why are you calling me?"

"Emma, Henny Inches and his wife just bought a new place off of Shore Road on Sunset Island. Next to someplace called Winterhaven," Mr. Cresswell said. "I'll be up this weekend! Didn't you get my note?"

"No, I didn't get any—"

"I sent it on Tuesday," her dad said. "You'll probably get it today. Listen, honey, I've got to run to a meeting, but I'm looking forward to seeing you!"

"Dad! Wait!" Emma said, "I'm going camping today, I won't be back until tomorrow afternoon—late."

"Then I'll see you then," her dad said. "Bye!"

"Bye, Dad," Emma answered.

She sat there a moment, staring into space. *So. My father is coming to the island for the weekend,* she thought. *He's borrowing some rich people's house. Of course, Dad could buy this island a few times over, so he doesn't really need the Inches's house at all to make the trip. He's certainly never wanted to come visit me here before. I wonder what—*

"Emma!" Ethan yelled from downstairs, interrupting Emma's thoughts. "C'mon! We're loading the van!"

"Be right there!" Emma yelled down. She reached for her purse, and then realized something: her father hadn't mentioned whether he was coming alone or with someone.

"What should I do?" Emma asked when she got downstairs.

"Pack the stuff in the corner," Jane said as she dropped another load into the back of the minivan they'd rented.

"Mom, what if I hurl, too?" Ethan asked anxiously. "Whenever I even hear about someone tossing their cookies it makes me feel like—"

"You're fine," Ethan," Jane said. She turned to Emma. "Wills is upstairs with some kind of stomach thing," she explained. "I'm pretty sure it was what he ate yesterday at Stinky Stein's house, because Stinky's got it, too."

"Yeah, but what if I'm not fine and we're, like, out on the highway?" Ethan asked. "I'm not barfing on the highway—"

Jane turned to her eldest son. She felt his forehead. "How do you feel?"

"Kind of funny," Ethan said guardedly.

"Ethan, Wills ate something that disagreed with him," his mother said. "You didn't eat it, so you're not going to get sick."

"I just hope you're sure about that," Ethan said.

"I'll pack some plastic bags, just in case," Emma offered, heading into the house. She took some plastic bags from the kitchen and when she came back out she found Sam and Allie in the driveway.

"Does this time of day actually exist?" Sam asked Emma from behind her leopard-print sunglasses.

"Evidently," Emma said. "And imagine you being here to witness it!"

"I have a new manifesto," Sam said. "If I'm awake before ten A.M., it should be because I haven't gone to sleep yet from the night before."

Emma grinned. "Aren't you going to help Jane load the van?"

Sam shook her head slowly. "I offered, but she said I should just stay out of her way. I took her advice. I must say, you're the height of outdoors fashion," she added.

"It was the best I could come up with," Emma said simply. She had on, in addition to the borrowed hiking boots, a pair of faded blue jeans, an oversize men's white

T-shirt, and a Baltimore Orioles baseball cap.

"It's the cap that makes it," Sam said. "What do you think of my uni?"

"Very, well, military," Emma said cautiously, regarding Sam's army-issue fatigue pants, camouflage shirt, and bush hat.

"In case I need to duck into the forest to hide from Allie, I want to be ready," Sam said emphatically.

"Speaking of Allie, where is she?"

"Inside with Ethan," Sam said, "getting in one last game of Nintendo."

"No Nintendo on Mount Washington," Emma replied. "No electricity."

"So how am I supposed to blow-dry my hair?" Sam asked.

Emma threw her a look.

"It was a joke," Sam said. "You remember humor, don't you?"

Ethan and Allie appeared in the doorway. Emma shook her head when she saw Allie's camping clothes—a pair of cutoff shorts and a bare-midriff white top. Ethan, on the other hand, was more conventionally dressed—camping shorts with about a million pockets, a bush shirt, and a floppy hat.

"Those clothes aren't going to give you much protection, Allie, if we happen to run into a bear," Jane called out to her as she slammed shut the back door of the minivan.

"Bear?" Allie asked. "There are bears where we're going? Like, actual bears?"

"Huge ones," Jane replied. "Very ferocious."

"Hey, it's been real," Allie said, backing toward the car Sam had driven over to the Hewitts', "but I'm outta here."

"Hold on, Girl Scout," Sam said, jumping to her feet. "If I'm going, you're going."

"But I'm too young to die young!" Allie cried dramatically.

"Not many bears this time of year," Ethan said, eyeing Allie's sexy outfit out of the corner of his eye. "I read it in *National Geographic.*"

"Can you all kindly get in the van so we can get going?" Jane asked.

With varying amounts of enthusiasm, the motley crew of would-be mountain climbers climbed into the minivan for the drive to New Hampshire—the first leg of their assault on fabled Mount Washington.

"I really think I have to barf, Mom,"

Ethan yelled from the back of the van when they were on the highway.

Emma handed him one of the plastic bags.

"I'm not blowing chunks in front of everyone into a plastic bag!" he yelled.

"Should I pull over?" Jane sighed.

Ethan thought a minute. "No, not yet. I'm okay. It could be soon, though."

"Eeeewww! Get away from me!" Allie shrieked, moving as far away from Ethan as she could.

"Are we having fun yet?" Sam muttered to no one in particular. She settled her head back against the seat and tried to find a comfortable position. "Wake me when it's over."

"Pinkham Notch, one mile," Ethan read the sign.

"That means we're almost there," Jane said. She wended the van along a winding mountain road.

"These curvy roads are making me feel kinda sick," Ethan warned.

He had been warning everyone of his impending stomach upheaval for more than two hours, but nothing had actually happened.

"Ethan," Allie said, "if you don't shut up about your stupid stomach I will punch you so hard you'll blow more than your cookies."

Ethan blushed bright red and stared out the window.

"Wow, it's really beautiful," Emma said, staring out the window. On both sides she could see the impressive peaks of the Presidential Range of the White Mountains. She was familiar with the Alps in Europe and the Rockies in the West, but had never seen the mountains of New Hampshire.

Jane slowed the car and pulled into a parking lot.

"Hey," Allie said. "There's lots of cars here."

"Mount Washington is a popular place," Jane said.

"Why does that car over there have a bumper sticker on it," Allie asked, "that says This Car Climbed Mount Washington?"

"There's an auto route to the top," Jane said as she undid her seat belt and started to get out of the van.

"Let's take that!" Allie said. "We can get

up and down really fast, and then be back at the island in time for dinner! I met this really cute guy who said he'd call me and—"

"Allie, give it a rest," Sam said.

"Yeah, like you really want to go up that mountain," Allie muttered darkly.

Jane looked in the back of the van at Allie. "Allie, please don't make me sorry I invited you," she said.

Now it was Allie's turn to blush. She looked belligerent, but didn't say anything.

"You guys stay here," Jane told them. "I've got to go check in at the ranger station." She walked over to a long log cabin with an American flag flying in front of it.

"What do you say we make a run for it?" Sam joked.

"Oh, sure, you're allowed to say stuff but I'm not," Allie groused.

Well, so far I was completely right, Emma thought. *This is a total disaster. And we haven't even gotten out of the van yet.*

Jane came back quickly, striding rapidly toward the van. "Okay," she said. "We're confirmed for the Hermit Lake shelter area. Let's get going."

They all climbed out of the van and put on their backpacks. Emma had packed hers the night before. In addition to her sleeping bag, she had some extra clothes, a flash-light, her mess kit, and some of the food they were going to have for dinner and for breakfast.

"This thing weighs a ton!" Sam complained, sliding into her backpack.

"Sam, can you carry mine?" Allie asked. Emma saw Sam shoot Allie a withering look.

"Just kidding!" Allie said.

"Which way, Mom?" Ethan asked Jane, who was busy studying a map.

"We're going up Tuckerman's Ravine," Jane said. "We just have to follow the signs. Don't forget to fill your canteens." She started walking toward a brown sign that said Tuckerman's Ravine Trail—To Summit.

Everyone had filled their canteens at a nearby water fountain, so they started following Jane. The trail led upward into the woods, and soon the parking lot at Pinkham Notch was far behind them.

"I don't think I've ever been so tired in my life," Sam said, gratefully unlacing her hiking boots and easing her feet into the cold water of Hermit Lake.

"But what about all that dance training?" Emma said, leaning over to unlace her own boots.

"Dance training is for dancing, a civilized activity engaged in by civilized people at a civilized hour of the day," Sam sniffed. "Mountain climbing is for burros, and last time I looked in the mirror, I was not a beast of burden."

Emma looked over at the backpack resting on the ground near Sam's side.

Sam looked at it, too. "I take that back," Sam said. "Today, I was a yak."

"That was some hike," Emma said, rolling her cramping shoulders.

"That wasn't a hike," Sam sniffed. "That was a death march!"

Emma looked around at her surroundings. The Hermit Lake campground was about two thirds of the way up Mount Washington, and was a crude—very crude, Emma thought—rest stop. There were no cabins, just some basic open-to-the-air shelters and some circles of stones where small camp fires could be built.

"Hi, guys," Ethan Hewitt said, sidling up to them. "Want some bug juice?" He indicated a container he was holding that contained some dubious-colored liquid.

"Some what?" Emma asked.

"Kool-Aid," Sam translated. "Usually with lots of critters floating in it."

"Pass," Emma said. "It's all yours!"

"Thanks!" Ethan said, taking a giant swig from the container.

"Where's Allie?" Sam asked Ethan.

"She's off exploring," Ethan said. "She asked me to come with her, but I was too tired."

"How about your mom?" Emma asked, swirling her feet around in the pond.

"Taking a nap," Ethan said simply. "But I'm gonna wake her up because she has to make dinner. There's Allie! Hey, Allie!"

At the far end of Hermit Lake, Emma could just make out the form of Allie Jacobs. She seemed to be looking for something along the shore of the pond. Then she slowly made her way over to where Sam and Emma were resting.

"Hey, guys," Allie grinned.

Emma looked at her. Halfway up the mountain, Allie had decided to change clothes, and now she looked a lot more like a hiker and a lot less like someone going to spend the day at the mall. She had on black jeans, a black-and-white checked work shirt, and had tied a red bandanna around her neck. Even Emma had to admit that she looked really cute.

"Hi, Allie," Sam said. "What've you got in the bag?" Allie was carrying a brown paper bag with her.

"Blueberries!" she said. "Look!"

Emma and Sam peered inside. Sure enough, the bag had what looked like several hundred fresh blueberries in it.

"They are blueberries, aren't they?" Allie asked. "I mean, these puppies aren't poisonous, are they?"

"They sure look like blueberries to me," Emma said.

"Cool!" Allie said. "So I'll rinse 'em off and we can eat 'em!"

"I thought you hated the woods," Sam said, looking at her queerly.

"Well, I did," Allie said. "But now I don't." With that logic behind her, she walked away from them.

"Strange kid," Sam said. "Really, really strange."

"I think she decided she hated all of this before she ever tried it," Emma guessed.

"We're looking at an outdoors convert!"

"Anybody want to do a trail with me?" Allie called to them.

"This is like discovering the eighth wonder of the world, or something!" Sam marveled.

"We're tired, thanks anyway!" Emma called back to Allie.

"You just never know," Sam said with a laugh.

By the time Emma and Sam had finished soaking their feet and had made their way back to the camping area, Jane Hewitt, Ethan, and Allie were already well on the way to whipping up a camp dinner.

"Hi!" Jane said, greeting them. "Allie did most of this," she added significantly, pointing to the dinner preparations.

"Is this amazing or what?" Emma whispered to Sam.

"I think the solution is to keep her in the woods forever," Sam whispered back. "She's a regular Ranger Rick."

"Dinner's ready, you guys," Allie said as Sam and Emma approached. "Here you go."

"Not to be rude or anything, but what is this slop?" Sam asked, giving a disbelieving look at the mess plate Allie handed her.

"It's good!" Jane said.

"That remains to be seen," Sam said, "but would you mind identifying it first?"

Jane grinned. "Freeze-dried meat stew. Freeze-dried mashed potatoes. Freeze-dried applesauce. Just add water!"

"What's to drink?" Sam cracked. "Freeze-dried water?"

"Have to travel light when you're back-packing," Jane said.

"Can't they have room service up here?" Sam joked. "Emma's going nuts without it."

"Sam, that's not true," Emma said, gamely taking a bite of meat stew. *It tastes like reconstituted mud,* she thought, gulping down a bite.

"Mmmm, not bad," Sam said, digging in to her plate of food.

"This proves my theory that you will eat and enjoy anything labeled Food," Emma laughed at Sam.

"And there are blueberries for dessert!" Allie reminded them.

As they ate, the sun was already starting to set, and the wind was picking up. Ethan put another spruce log on the fire, and they all huddled closer to its warmth.

"Yuck!" Sam said. "What stinks?" She wrinkled her nose and looked at Allie sitting next to her.

"You must be talking about my insect repellent," Allie said. "Some cool guys camping near the pond gave it to me. It's called Real Campers."

"It should be called Death by Asphyxiation," Sam said. "Man, that's some vile stuff."

"At least I'm not getting bitten," Allie said loftily. "You'll see what it's like—those guys told me. After dinner, huge clouds of mosquitoes rise up from the pond and descend on the campsite like bloodsuckers, and then—"

"Allie!" Sam stopped her before she could get on too big a roll.

"Anyway," Allie said, "you and Emma get to see this for yourselves. Because since we made dinner, you two get to clean up."

"Those are the rules," Jane agreed, looking over at Emma.

"What were you saying before about room service, Sam?" Emma joked.

The girls laughed, and started to gather up the tin dinner plates.

* * *

"It is major freezing," Sam said, snuggling down deeper into her sleeping bag. "Whoever decided it was fun to sleep outside?"

It was nearly ten o'clock, the dishes had long been done, and Sam and Emma were curled up in their sleeping bags in one of the lean-to shelters at Hidden Lake. There literally was nothing else to do.

"Good question," Emma agreed, shivering inside her sleeping bag.

"Of course," Sam cracked, "it wouldn't be nearly as cold if Kurt was here."

"I wish," Emma murmured dreamily. "Don't you wish Pres were here?"

"Gee, no, I'd much rather be with Allie Jacobs," Sam said, dead-pan.

The two of them were quiet for a moment, listening to the chirping of the crickets and the cackle of a still-burning campfire.

"Did I tell you my father was coming to Sunset Island this weekend?" Emma asked.

"The Boston Baron himself? The lover of young ladies only barely older than ourselves?" Sam joked.

Emma sighed. *Can I help it if after my*

mother and my father split up, he decided that what he needed to renew his life was a girlfriend half his age?

"Well, she did break up with him," Emma reminded.

"There'll be a replacement," Sam prophesied. "Mark my words."

"How do you know?" Emma said. "Maybe he's changed."

"Do I know men or do I know men?" Sam said.

"Not as well as you pretend to know them," Emma said pointedly.

"Well, if that was a little dig at my continued status as the oldest living virgin," Sam said, "let me remind you that you are second in line!"

"Maybe not for long," Emma said.

Sam stuck her head out of her sleeping bag. "You have dirt to tell me?"

"Not really," Emma replied. "I just think that if I'm really going to join the Peace Corps and go to Africa, I might just, you know, kind of seal my relationship with Kurt before I go."

"Listen, Em, I'm all for you doing the deed with Kurt," Sam said, "but I don't know if that's a good reason. I mean, you have this big moment, and then you fly off into the sunset?"

"Well, I'm only just beginning to think about it!" Emma defended herself.

"Oh, come on," Sam chided her. "You've been thinking about the horizontal bop with Kurt forever. You just haven't been doing it."

"That's true," Emma conceded. "But then, neither have you."

"Only because I haven't found the perfect candidate," Sam assured her. "When I do, me and Mr. Stud Puppet will disappear to some romantic hideaway for a few days and not come up for air."

"Mmmmm," Emma murmured noncommittally. *Sometimes I wonder if Sam is even more afraid of love than I am,* she thought to herself.

"Anyway, listen, concerning your dear old dad," Sam said, changing the subject, "I predict that Pops is not coming to Sunset Island to visit his daughter by his lonesome, if you catch my drift."

"Consider it caught," Emma replied softly.

Emma closed her eyes and tried to sleep,

but couldn't help thinking that Sam was probably right, and that if her father was bringing a female companion, she was probably closer to her age than his own.

FOUR

"Geez, it's cold," Sam said, shivering in her sleeping bag and snuggling deeper into the floor of the shelter early the next morning.

"You said something like that right before you went to sleep last night," Emma replied, rubbing her eyes sleepily.

"So, I'm consistent," Sam said, her voice muffled by the bag that she had pulled up over her head. "What time is it?"

Emma looked at her watch. "Six forty-five in the morning."

"*Six forty-five?*" Sam yelped. "There are only two things in the world that I should be doing at that hour, and both of them involve my bed!"

Emma laughed. She peered out. She could see that Allie and Ethan were already up and dressed, and were diligently adding kindling to a small fire they had gotten going in the fire pit.

"Allie and Ethan are up," Emma reported.

"Good," Sam said. "I'm down. Remind me never to sleep on the hard ground again." Emma watched Sam inch even deeper into her mummy-style bag. "I'm never getting out of this sleeping bag, I just want you to know that. Brrrrr!"

Can't say as I blame her, Emma thought. *You can see your breath, and it's the middle of the summer. I don't think I'd like to be up here in mid-January. Not my idea of a good time.*

"Good morning, girls!" Emma saw Jane Hewitt stick her head into their shelter.

"Hi, Jane," Emma said. "Sleep okay?"

"Remind me never to sleep in a lean-to again," Jane grimaced, gingerly massaging a knot out of her left shoulder with her right hand. "I forgot what it's like."

"Gee, I said the same thing," Sam marveled, "and it's definitely worth forgetting."

Emma sat up and stretched. "God, it really is freezing."

"I'm never, never, never getting up!" Sam sang from inside her bag.

"You have to," Jane said. "Bad news."

Sam sat up quickly. "Don't tell me," she said, "we're expanding our camping trip to a week because Allie loves it so much!"

"Worse than that," Jane said. "The ranger station sent up word that they're expecting some bad weather on the mountain this afternoon. We've got to cut our trip short."

"Gee, bummer," Sam said with a big grin on her face.

Jane laughed. "Okay, I know you aren't exactly having the time of your life, but Allie really loves it, and even Ethan has come around. It's too bad we have to end this, for their sakes."

"Yeah," Sam agreed, trying to look solemn.

"How bad is the weather supposed to get?" Emma said. Kurt had told her that there were times, even during the summer, where the upper part of the mountain was closed because of fog, cold, and sometimes even snow.

"Bad," Jane said bluntly. "It might snow."

"Snow in the middle of summer?" Sam queried. "Mondo-bizarro!"

"It happens up here," Jane said. "So, let's get cracking." Jane left to see about the kids.

"We're outta here! Hurray!" Sam cried exuberantly, jumping out of the sleeping bag.

"Nice outfit," Emma commented. She could see that Sam had gone to sleep in the same clothes she had worn the day before.

"I believe in recycling," Sam said. "I'm an environmental kind of babe." She ran her tongue around the inside of her mouth. "Yuck. It feels like furry creatures nested in here overnight."

"Breakfast's ready!" Allie Jacobs's voice sang out from the area where she and Ethan had built their fire.

"Yum. My favorite words!" Sam said, rubbing her arms briskly.

"For you it's the call of the wild," Emma said with a laugh.

"Do you know how many calories I must have burned off yesterday?" Sam asked indignantly. "Freeze-dried eggs, here I come!"

"Thanks, Mrs. Hewitt," Allie Jacobs said as she stood in the Hewitts' driveway. They had just arrived back on the island. For most of the drive back Allie had been talking about how cool the trip had been. "It was really fun."

"You're welcome, Allie," Jane said with a twinkle in her eye, "I think you've found your calling in life."

Emma, who had slept in the car for most of the way back to Sunset Island, climbed groggily out of the van.

"It was kinda, you know, cool," Allie said, trying to appear nonchalant. "So, do you want to plan another trip sometime soon? A longer one?"

"Ahhhhhhhh!" Sam screamed, and pretended to strangle Allie.

"You don't have to come next time," Allie told Sam. "Right, Jane?" Allie asked.

"And neither do you," Ethan told Emma, sidling over next to Allie.

"Well, we'll see," Jane hedged. "Anyway, I'm really glad you enjoyed it."

"I'll call you later," Sam promised Emma. "When's your dad coming?"

Emma shrugged. "He might be here already," she said. "Then again, maybe not."

That might be best, Emma thought, *if he had a quick change of mind and decided not to come at all. I'm not so sure I can take all this family bonding stuff. Not with* my *family!*

"Whatever," Sam said, "I'm too tired to think."

"Call me," Emma said with a grin, "when you wake up."

"That might be next week," Sam retorted, pulling her bag out of the back of the minivan.

"See you, Sam," Jane said. "You guys ready to unpack the van?"

"Sure," Emma said, even though it was about the last thing on earth she felt like doing at that moment. But she cheerfully helped unload everything, and then headed upstairs for a long hot bath.

I'm not even checking to see if my father is here until I wash this grunge off of myself, Emma decided, dropping her clothes in the hamper. *In the words of Sam Bridges, when it comes to travel, I think from now on I'll stick to four-star hotels.*

An hour later, when Emma felt clean and reasonably human again, she threw on some cotton shorts and a T-shirt and went downstairs. There was a note from Jeff for her on the counter.

Emma,
Your dad called and said he won't be here until late tonight, about 10:30 he thinks.

Jeff

Next to Jeff's note was a letter from her father, postmarked from Miami, Florida—his most recent home.

Since the house was quiet (she figured everyone was taking a nap) Emma ran back up to her room and opened the letter.

Dear Emma,

Great news! I've been invited to spend the weekend at Henny Inches' new place on your island. I didn't think I would get to see you again so quickly, but it's wonderful we will be able to get together at least twice this summer.

It meant a great deal to me to have dinner with you on Paradise Island. You are turning into an outstanding young woman.

Two other exciting things I want to tell you about. First, work. You know that since your mother and I divorced, I've pretty much been retired. But now an investment group here has been trying to convince me to join them in a venture capital operation, and I'm going to do it. I miss the excitement.

Second, I have met a lovely young woman named Princess-Alexis Baltres. You will get to meet her this coming weekend.

I can't wait to see you.

Dad

Two points for Sam, Emma thought grimly. *I couldn't have imagined that my father could find himself a new girlfriend in just a few weeks, but I guess parents are capable of anything. Especially mine. The good news is that he called her a woman. Maybe this time she won't be young enough to be my big sister.*

Emma felt depression surround her like a curtain. She lay down on her bed and stared at the ceiling. *Okay, Emma, why do you feel so awful?* she asked herself. *Figure it out.*

Because . . . because . . . because I'm disappointed that my father isn't making a trip just to see me, instead of to show off his latest bimbette, she realized.

She reached into the drawer of her night-stand and took out the diary her aunt Liz had given her the summer before, hoping to write down what she was feeling. But no matter how hard she tried, she didn't feel like writing.

I wish I didn't feel so bad about him coming here, Emma thought, doodling in the corner of a page of her diary. *Maybe I'll call Carrie, see if she has any words of advice.*

She reached for the phone by her bed and dialed Carrie at the Templetons.

"Hello, this is Carrie Alden," Carrie said, answering the phone.

"Hi, Car," Emma said, immediately feeling a little better at just hearing her friend's voice. "It's me."

"Hi, Emma," Carrie said. "Sam just called me. I got the full report on your camping trip. Did Allie really turn into this gung ho camper?"

"She really did," Emma confirmed.

"Unbelievable," Carrie marveled.

"Listen," Emma said, "I wanted to talk to you about something."

"What's up?"

"I got a call from my dad right before we left to go camping," Emma said. "He's coming to the island. Tonight."

"I know," Carrie replied. "Sam told me about it."

"Well, the thing is," Emma said, leaning up against the pillows on her bed, "I'm not really looking forward to seeing him. I don't think so, anyway."

"Do you know why?" Carrie asked reasonably.

"Kind of," Emma said. "I mean, the last time I saw him was on Paradise Island, and remember I told you how my father and I agreed we were going to try to get to know each other better. But he's never made any effort since then. . . ."

"Well, maybe he is now," Carrie said.

"Carrie, he's bringing some princess with him," Emma said with disgust. "He wrote me about her in a letter. He's not coming just to visit me. He just wants to show off his latest young girlfriend."

"Just because he's coming with someone doesn't mean he isn't coming to see you," Carrie replied.

Emma thought about that for a moment. "I suppose," she sighed.

"Maybe it'll be really great," Carrie said.

"I don't think so," Emma stated bluntly.

"I was thinking," Carrie mused, "maybe you're kind of glad and mad at the same time."

"Meaning?" Emma asked.

"Meaning that while part of you is glad that he's trying to make contact with you again, another part of you is mad for all those years he ignored you."

"Hmmm," Emma said. "That actually might make sense."

"So, between that and him bringing some stranger with him, you have a lot to feel upset about," Carrie concluded.

"Carrie Alden, you amaze me," Emma said. "I'm truly impressed. Have you ever thought about becoming a shrink?"

Carrie laughed. "My bill is already in the mail!"

Emma hung up, feeling much better about life in general. *Carrie is really smart and insightful,* Emma thought, heading downstairs.

"Hi, there," Jeff Hewitt said when he saw Emma. "I just came down a few minutes ago. A delivery came for you."

"Me?" Emma said.

"Yep," Jeff said. "Flowers. Your name's on the card. Look in the dining room."

Emma went quickly into the dining room. On the table was a handpicked arrangement of wildflowers and roses, in a clear glass vase. Emma picked up the card that came with the flowers and read it.

Emma,
Welcome home flowers for the queen of Mount Washington. My dad caught sea trout—what say you come for dinner at 7:30 tonight? I'm cooking!
Kurt

Emma smiled broadly when she read the card. *Dinner with Kurt? Kurt cooking? Sounds great.*

Emma cleared it with Jeff, who told her that she could have the night off.

"Oh, one other thing," Emma said, stopping on her way back upstairs. "If my father calls please tell him I'm having dinner with my boyfriend and that I'll call him in the morning."

Emma thought she saw Jeff give her an odd look.

"You're going to make your dad wait—"

"Please, Jeff," Emma said. "Tell him I'll call him in the morning."

"It's your life," Jeff said with a shrug.

Emma went back upstairs to get ready for a romantic dinner with Kurt.

It is my life, Emma thought defiantly as she got ready for her date with Kurt. *I don't have to plan my life around being at his— and his latest bimbo's—beck and call. I'm going to be with Kurt, and I'm going to have a wonderful time.*

And I'm not going to think about my father at all.

FIVE

"Kurt," Emma said, "you're a guy of many talents." She looked with approval at the table that he had set out on the small back patio of his family's somewhat run-down house.

"And I'm a terrific cook, too," Kurt said as he expertly maneuvered a couple of foil-wrapped packages on the charcoal grill.

"And modest," Emma added. "Don't forget modest."

"That goes without saying," Kurt grinned. He took a sip from a can of beer.

And handsome. Unbelievably handsome, Emma thought.

Even though he wore nothing more elaborate than a pair of faded jeans and a long-sleeved red cotton T-shirt, Emma found him irresistibly good-looking.

I can't stand beer, but I even like the way he drinks from the can.

"So your dad caught these fish?" Emma asked as she sat down at the candle-lit table, a glass of sparkling water in her hand.

"Yep," Kurt said. "It's called sea trout."

As Kurt told her about his father's fishing expedition (Kurt's dad was a professional fisherman), she sipped the water slowly.

There was a time I would have wanted a glass of wine—or two or three—, Emma thought, remembering the summer before when she had started drinking and it had gotten out of hand. She also remembered how a friend had been killed in a car accident after only a modest amount of drinking. Emma shivered and put down her glass.

"So," Kurt was concluding, "all in all Dad had a great day on the water."

"What is a sea trout, exactly?" Emma asked, snapping back to the present.

"It's not the real name," Kurt explained as he fiddled with the foil packages again.

"Their real name is weakfish, but some marketing genius in New York decided that no one would buy a fish called a weakfish."

"Some marketing genius was right," Emma laughed.

Kurt lifted the foil packages off the grill and put them on a serving plate. He and Emma had already eaten a green salad and a bowl of fresh Maine steamers, but Emma was still incredibly hungry—unusual for her.

Must be all that mountain climbing, she thought to herself with a grin.

"Hope you like it, babe!" Kurt said, setting the serving plate on the table. "It has an exotic name—Kurt's Weakfish Surprise."

Kurt took a knife and cut into the foil packages. Instantly the most wonderful aroma filled the air—steamed fresh fish, garlic, onion, green pepper, and what looked like wild mushrooms.

"Looks edible," Emma teased.

"I'm not done yet," Kurt said. He dashed into the house and came out with a small covered dish.

"Mmmm," Emma murmured. "Fresh corn, my favorite."

"Well, dig in," Kurt said with a boyish grin.

"Bon appetit," Emma answered. She took a bite of the fish. "Kurt, it's great! Where'd you learn to cook?"

"My dad," Kurt said.

"He taught you?" Emma queried.

"Yep, he's pretty handy in the kitchen."

Emma took another bite of the fish. "He must be a pretty good teacher," she commented.

"Nah," Kurt said with a grin, "I'm just a great student."

"I didn't know your dad could cook," Emma noted. "I thought all he did was grimace every time you mention my name."

Kurt laughed uncomfortably. "You just don't understand," he said.

"Don't understand what?" Emma asked.

"How Mainers are," Kurt said matter-of-factly, pouring himself a glass of iced tea and taking a sip.

"Is that so?" Emma asked. "I know that he's not particularly gracious around me."

"He's not particularly gracious, as you put it, around strangers in general," Kurt explained.

"And I'm a stranger?" Emma asked,

sounding hurt. "I thought I was your girlfriend!"

"Emma," Kurt explained coolly, "around these parts, a stranger is anyone whose grandparents weren't born in Maine."

"But that is just so unfair!" Emma exclaimed, a touch of anger in her voice.

"Hey, my father's not your boyfriend," Kurt responded. "I am."

"But at least he could be civil to me," Emma pointed out, her anger receding somewhat. "He acts like I don't exist."

"He *is* being civil to you," Kurt explained, starting to smile a bit. "You should see him if you're on his bad list."

"Spare me," Emma pleaded. "Just don't take after him, okay?"

"I won't," Kurt said. "I *like* beautiful girls from Boston."

"He should, too," Emma replied. "I'm extremely likable."

"You scare him," Kurt responded.

Emma sighed and put down her fork. "The stupid money thing, right?"

Kurt shrugged. "From his point of view it's not so stupid. He's afraid I'll leave the island because of you and your evil, contaminated millions."

"That's ridiculous!" Emma said.

"I'm not saying he's right," Kurt said directly, "that's just the way that he feels."

"Can't you talk to him?"

Kurt laughed again. "Another thing about Mainers," he said, "is that they're really stubborn. Look up the word 'stubborn' in the dictionary—my dad's picture is the definition."

"Just don't turn out like him," Emma repeated, mock sternly.

"Yes ma'am," Kurt said obediently. "Now, eat your fish like a good girl."

Emma stuck her tongue out at Kurt and then continued eating. They stayed on safe topics until they'd both finished dinner.

"How about dessert?" Kurt asked, wiping his mouth with his napkin.

"I'm stuffed!" Emma protested.

"Better not be," Kurt warned. He picked up both their plates and disappeared into the kitchen. A moment later he came out with two steaming pieces of apple pie, each covered with a scoop of vanilla ice cream.

"That looks great," Emma commented as Kurt set her plate down in front of her.

"It is," Kurt said simply.

"Your dad taught you to bake, too?"

Emma asked incredulously.

"Are you kidding?" Kurt answered. "Rubie gave me this when I told her you were coming over for dinner." Rubie was Kurt's boisterous adopted aunt who owned the best workingman's seafood restaurant on the island.

Emma laughed. "That's cheating!""

"That's the truth," Kurt noted with a twinkle in his eyes.

"Speaking of dads," Kurt continued, "I hope I'm going to meet yours soon. Like tomorrow."

"Who told you he was coming?" Emma asked, surprised.

"Sam," Kurt answered.

"Yes," Emma sighed, "he'll be here tomorrow."

Actually, he's probably on the island already, but I'd rather be right where I am than with my dad.

"You promise he'll be civil to me?" Kurt joked.

"Oh, he'll be civil," Emma sighed again. "Cresswells are *always* civil."

"You don't talk much about him," Kurt noted.

"You're right," Emma said quietly.

"Why?"

"There's not much to talk about," Emma replied, dipping her spoon into the vanilla ice cream. "I don't know him very well, and he certainly doesn't know me."

"Like your mom?" Kurt asked.

Emma remembered Kurt's horrible impression of her mother when Kat had ridden in Kurt's taxi, and she winced at the memory.

"Different," Emma mused. "I actually kind of like my dad. At least I feel like I could like him. When I was a kid he was always at work—I never really saw him."

"That's a drag," Kurt commented.

Emma nodded. "He married rich, and then I think he felt like he had to prove to my mother that he could make his own fortune. Which he did, I might add."

"Two, two, two fortunes in one!" Kurt quipped. "And you're an only child who inherits everything. Hey, I bet Sam wants to marry you!"

Emma swatted his arm. "I'd like to know my dad better—I mean, I feel like there might be an actual person there worth knowing—"

"Unlike your mother," Kurt added.

"Right," Emma agreed. "Remember I told you that when I saw him in Paradise Island he said he was going to make this big effort to really get to know me?"

Kurt nodded and finished his pie.

"Well, I haven't heard from him since. Until now, that is."

"So maybe this is the effort," Kurt said.

"That's what Carrie said," Emma replied. "But he's bringing his latest concubine with him. Some kind of princess who is probably young enough for us to double-date."

"A lot of men have girlfriends half their age," Kurt pointed out.

"Not you," Emma joked.

"I have better taste," Kurt replied.

"Well, I suppose ten is a little too young anyway!" Emma joked.

"You'd rather your father didn't come?" Kurt asked.

"Maybe," Emma said. "Or maybe I'd just rather he come alone."

"Hey, I've got an idea," Kurt said impetuously. "Why don't we introduce my father to your father?"

"You're joking," Emma asked.

God, I hope he's joking.

"The poor-but-honest downeast Mainer

fisherman meets the divorced Boston investment banker now living the life of luxury in sunny Florida," Kurt rhapsodied.

"Great idea," Emma laughed. "A real Sunset Island love fest."

"You never know," Kurt said. "Maybe they'd like each other."

"Maybe," Emma said, playing along. "But I doubt it."

I can't think of any two people who have less in common than Kurt's dad and my father. It's hard to believe that they even live in the same country!

"Well," Kurt said, "maybe we can introduce him to Rubie," Kurt offered. "She's always interested in handsome older men."

Emma laughed. "Now, if my dad would take up with Rubie, he'd be showing some taste for a change!"

"So, here's the deal," Kurt said. "If this princess person is awful, we give her the wrong directions to somewhere or other, and then whisk your dad away to rendezvous with Rubie!"

"Great idea," Emma agreed coyly, "but it's not a deal until it's sealed."

"So seal it," Kurt said.

Emma stood up, walked over to Kurt, and kissed him.

The kiss was every bit as delicious as dinner had been.

"Swimmers, take your mark," Kurt shouted from the side of the Sunset Country Club's outdoor pool. A row of eight- and nine-year-old boys lined up to race the twenty-five-yard freestyle event.

It was the next morning—Sunday morning—and Emma was chaperoning Wills and Ethan Hewitt at the swim meet that had been organized against a Y.M.C.A. from Wells, a small town near Algonquin.

Kurt blew a shrill whistle and the first set of kids jumped into the pool.

Emma put on her sunglasses and hugged her knees to her chest as she watched the race from her chaise lounge. It was difficult for her to concentrate on it, since her father was going to show up any minute. Brent Cresswell had called Emma earlier that morning and arranged to meet her at the club—he had reciprocal privileges there from his country club in Florida.

"Faster, Wills! Pull!" Ethan screamed to his brother in the water.

"C'mon, Tommy! *Go!*" Kids were lined up along the side of the pool, screaming at their friends to swim faster.

Emma looked down at the conservative but classy blue one-piece bathing suit she'd chosen. *Since Dad's bimbettes parade around in postage-stamp-sized frilled bikinis, the least I can do is show this one what good taste is,* Emma thought, straightening one narrow strap.

"Wills, go for it!" Ethan yelled to his brother. "Hurry up! Go, go, go!"

Emma looked at Wills thrashing through the water. He appeared to be going as fast as he could. Which unfortunately was not particularly fast.

Kurt blew the whistle, signaling a winner. Wills made his touch at the end of the pool, finishing fifth or sixth out of the eight swimmers.

"Wills, you suck!" Ethan yelled as his brother climbed out of the pool and walked wearily, dripping and shivering, back to where Ethan and Emma were sitting.

"I do not!" Wills said.

"Uh huh!" Ethan taunted. "You are so slow!"

"Am not!"

"Are so. You swim like a turtle!"

"Oh, yeah?" Wills shot back. "Well . . . well, at least I don't have zits. You have zits on your chin!"

"Shut up!" Ethan yelled, his voice cracking.

"And your back!" Wills added, knowing he'd scored big points.

Nice comeback, Wills. Two points for you. But I think it's time for the mature au pair in charge of peacekeeping to step in here, Emma thought.

"Uh, Ethan?" Emma ventured.

"Yeah?"

"Maybe you'd better chill out until after you swim your race," Emma suggested.

"Why?" Ethan responded. "Everything I'm saying is true!"

"Is *not*!" Wills wailed.

"Is too!" Ethan taunted again. "Wills finished last, Wills finished last!"

"I was not *last*!" Wills cried.

This is quickly getting out of control. It's hard to believe that this morning these two were the best of friends at the breakfast table.

"Were too!" Ethan repeated.

"Oh, yeah?" Wills shot back. "I creamed you at Nintendo."

Emma knew this was true. All of a sudden Ethan got very quiet.

"Uh, Ethan," Emma spoke up, "You don't want to tire yourself out before your race. Go buy yourself a soda." She handed Ethan a dollar.

He took it and started walking toward the snack bar.

"Can I have a soda, too?" Wills looked forlornly at Emma.

"Don't worry about the race," Emma said to him, trying to cheer him up.

"But I stunk!" Wills admitted. "By the time I made the touch, they were starting the next group!"

Wills was trying hard not to cry. Emma felt bad for the sweet kid, who loved to swim and really wanted to be good at it.

"The important thing is that you tried," Emma told him gently.

Wills made a face. "That's what grown-ups always say."

"Well, it's true—kind of," Emma said lamely.

"It doesn't matter who wins or loses, it's

how you play the game." Wills singsonged something his dad had told him a thousand times. "But it does too matter! Everyone likes you if you win, and everyone says you're a dweeb if you lose!"

"It really is easier to win, isn't it," Emma agreed.

Wills nodded miserably.

"Well, maybe you'd like to have more private lessons with Kurt," Emma suggested.

Wills's face lit up. "You think I could?"

"I'll talk to your parents about it," Emma promised. "Now, go get yourself a soda, too." Wills took the dollar Emma gave him and headed off to the main building.

"Very nicely done, Emma," a familiar male voice said to her. "You'll make a good parent someday."

Emma turned toward the voice. It wasn't one she heard very often.

It was her father.

And standing next to her father was a tall, tanned, extremely pretty young woman with long blond hair cascading down her back. She wore tight cigarette-style black jeans, a sleeveless white mock turtleneck, big hoop earrings, and absolutely flawless makeup.

That must be the princess, Emma thought. *Princess Alexis Baltres. That's weird, I know her from somewhere. From television? Magazines? The movies? She looks so familiar and I just can't place her.*

"Hello, Dad," Emma said, getting up to give her father an awkward hug.

Her father hugged her warmly. "I want to introduce you two," he said with a proud grin. "This is my daughter, Emma, and this"—he turned to look at the gorgeous, statuesque blonde admiringly—"*this* . . . is Princess-Alexis."

SIX

"A pleasure to meet you, Princess Alexis," Emma said coolly, reaching her hand out to the princess.

Big deal, it's not like I haven't met royalty before, Emma thought to herself. *I sat with Princess Di at Wimbledon one year—I am not impressed.*

The exquisitely lovely blond girl with the perfect features and ice-blue eyes—Emma figured that she couldn't be older than mid-twenties—took her hand and shook it limply.

"Charmed," Princess-Alexis said, making it clear she was bored out of her skull.

"What country are you from?" Emma

asked. She hadn't detected any accent in the one word Princess Alexis had uttered.

"New York," Princess-Alexis said, slightly adenoidally.

Emma pressed her lips together to suppress a snicker. "No, I mean, from what country is your royal title?"

Princess-Alexis eyed Emma's father coolly.

"Princess-Alexis isn't really royalty," Brent explained hastily. "It's a hyphenated name. You know. Princess-Alexis."

"On my comp cards is just says Princess, though," Princess-Alexis added.

"Comp cards," Emma repeated.

"I'm a model," Princess-Alexis explained.

"I never would have guessed," Emma said, managing to keep a straight face.

"Kind of smart thinking on her agent's part, don't you think?" Emma's father asked.

"I'm the only Princess listed in the *American Models' Directory,*" Princess reported proudly.

"Imagine!" Emma marveled. Out of the corner of her eye she could see Kurt Ackerman standing by the pool water fountain, watching the proceedings with interest.

This is really rich, Emma thought. *I wish I could tell Kurt about good ole Princess right this minute.*

"Your father has told me a lot about you," Princess said in a friendlier voice.

"Really?" Emma asked. "Like what?"

Princess looked puzzled. "Oh, you know . . . he must have said something . . ."

"He probably told you about all the time we've spent together over the years," Emma said blithely. "How we've become so close—"

"Yeah," Princess agreed brightly. "That was probably it!"

Emma's father had the good grace to look chagrined. Princess just looked at him and shrugged.

Emma studied the tall young woman. *I am just so sure that I know her from someplace, but I just can't place where.*

"You and Princess have a lot in common!" Brent said enthusiastically.

"Is that so?" Emma asked skeptically.

"Yes!" Brent assured his daughter.

"Do tell," Emma prompted unenthusiastically.

"You both went to Aubergame Academy,"

Brent said. "Princess was just a few years ahead of you."

A light bulb went on in Emma's head.

Of course, she thought. *That's where I know her from. Switzerland. Boarding school. She's Alexis Streicher—how'd her name become Baltres? She was four years ahead of me there. Oh, my God, she's the same age as Minnie Mouse. Her younger sister Gisela was in my year. Oh, yes! Alexis got kicked out of school for sleeping with the headmaster. I remember, it was a big scandal. I wonder if she's told my father about that.*

"Ah yes," Emma said politely, looking at Alexis. "I think your younger sister—"

"Gisella?" Princess queried.

"How is she?" Emma queried, trying to be well mannered.

"Married," Princess replied, flipping her blond hair back over her shoulders haughtily. "To Count Wilheim Austerbach, in Australia."

"Now, would that be a model with the hyphenated name Count-Wilheim, or would that be an actual count?" Emma asked seriously.

"My sister is now Countess Austerbach!"

Princess exclaimed haughtily.

"Well, congratulations! Give her my best," Emma said smoothly. "I hope she's worked on that New York accent of hers—I remember she never could quite get rid of it—people are so hard on royalty, you know."

"It's a small world," Brent said jovially.

"Yes it is," Emma agreed.

Now, time for me throw him my curve-ball.

"Dad, I'd like to introduce someone to *you,*" Emma said.

"My pleasure," Brent said, looking from side to side.

"Oh, Kurt?" Emma called to Kurt, who was still standing by the pool water fountain, smiling broadly.

Kurt Ackerman strode up to Emma and took her outstretched hand. He was wearing a pair of baggy light blue swim shorts and nothing else, and Emma thought he looked great.

"Yes, Emma?" he said confidently.

"Kurt, this is my father, Brent Cresswell, and his special friend Princess-Alexis Streicher Baltres," Emma announced. "Dad, Princess—my boyfriend, Kurt Ackerman."

Kurt stuck his hand out to Brent Cresswell. "Nice to meet you, sir," Kurt said politely.

"Call me Brent!" Emma's father chided him good-naturedly.

"Brent it is," Kurt repeated.

"Hi, Kurt," Emma heard Princess coo, reaching a perfectly manicured hand out to Kurt. "Please call me Princess."

"Nice to meet you, too, uh, Princess," Kurt said, shaking Princess's hand briefly.

"The pleasure's mine," Princess said, holding Kurt's hand a moment longer than she should have.

Oh, brother, Emma thought. She looked at her father to see if he noticed, but he was oblivious.

"Well," Kurt said, "I'm still working now so—"

"Wait!" Princess said. Emma watched her reach into her white quilted Chanel pocketbook and pull a three-by-five card out of it to give to Kurt.

"My composite card," Princess murmured significantly.

Kurt cocked his head quizzically.

"She only gives them to people she would

like as friends," Brent explained solemnly.

"Well, gee . . ." Kurt said. "That's . . . that's really swell." He nodded, and Emma could see he was trying hard not to laugh. He gave Emma a warm kiss, and then went over to the lifeguard stand by the pool.

"Nice fellow," Brent said to Emma.

"Very handsome," Princess said in a low voice. "Very."

Please spare me. If it turns out that my father's very special friend is going to put the moves on Kurt I am going to throw up, and I am going to aim for her, Emma thought nastily.

"Well, Dad," Emma said brightly, "I'm supposed to be working now, too, so—"

"Fine," Brent responded. "May Spencer-Rumsey is having us over this afternoon anyway."

She's the lady who runs Spencer Publishing, Emma thought, *the one who wanted Carrie to do the photos for her book about Sunset Island. And Carrie refused to do them because the book wouldn't paint an honest picture of the island.*

"Have fun," Emma said evenly.

"How about dinner tonight?" her dad asked her.

"Well—"

"Just the four of us?" he continued. "You, me, Princess, and Kurt?"

"Yes," Princess cooed again, "the *four* of us." She pronounced "four" as "fow-uh."

"Kurt's working," Emma responded. "He drives a cab."

"A cab?" Princess asked, wrinkling her perfect aquiline nose.

"Kurt's putting himself through college," Emma added.

"Oh, I see!" Princess replied, clearly relieved. "I knew he wasn't an ordinary cab-driver. I could tell just by looking."

"Could you?" Emma asked, murder in her heart.

"Absolutely," Princess assured her. "So . . . you're sure he can't get off tonight?"

"He takes his responsibilities seriously," Emma said in a steely voice.

"Oh, yeah," Princess agreed. "Well, on second thought, I think I'd rather just have a stroll through town."

Before this visit is over I am going to commit homicide, Emma thought, *and she is going to be the victim. My dad is completely oblivious to this tramp! She only wanted to have dinner with us because Kurt would be there.*

"Then it's just you and me," Brent said to his daughter.

Thrills, Emma thought. "Someplace you want to go?"

"How about the Sunset Inn? Henny said it's good," Brent responded.

I've got the night off, Emma said to herself. *I can't very well say no to my father.*

"Okay, I'll make a reservation for eight P.M.?" Emma offered.

"Great!" Brent said.

No, it's not great, Emma thought. *Not only do I wish you'd stayed in Florida, but I'm also going to have to keep watch on your special friend and my boyfriend. I don't think Kurt would do anything, but Princess doesn't strike me as a girl who takes no for an answer. She didn't seven years ago at boarding school, and some things do not change.*

"So," Brent said to his daughter when they were both seated at an outdoor table on the deck of the Sunset Inn, "here we are!"

Emma nodded.

"You look great," Brent told his daughter.

Emma had chosen a simple blue shift she had bought in Paris on her last trip there. The shift was exactly the same color as her eyes. The Hewitts had all whistled at her when she left their house to meet her father.

"Thanks, Dad," Emma replied.

"Do you want a drink?" Brent asked her lightly.

"I'll pass," Emma answered coolly.

"I'm having a martini," Brent pronounced. "A beautiful drink with my beautiful daughter."

Emma mustered a smile.

Okay, she told herself. *Just cut right to the chase with him, as Sam would say. Tell him what you think of his Princess, or else you are going to have an awful time every minute that he's on this island.*

"How was your afternoon?" Emma asked politely, after her father had his drink brought to him.

"Fine," Brent said, "lovely people."

"Dad, can I ask you something serious?" Emma asked cautiously.

This is not at all my style.

"Sure, sweetheart," Brent said, "anything. We decided we were going to get to know each other."

"It's about Princess," Emma said.

"Oh!" Brent laughed. "You want to know how we met!"

"Well, that's part of it but—"

"Sunshine National Bank in Miami," Brent said, "gave this party for the investment community a few weeks back."

"Princess is in the investment community?" Emma asked in an astonished tone of voice.

Her father laughed. "No," he said. "They put on a fashion show afterward—Princess was one of the models."

"So you met at the party," Emma said evenly.

"Something like that," her father replied. "What's the matter, did she make a bad impression?"

"Dad, she was all over my boyfriend!" Emma exclaimed, much louder than she intended.

Look at him, Emma thought. *He's smiling.*

"That's just her way," Brent said.

"Her way of *what?*" Emma queried pointedly.

"How she deals with people," her father explained. "Actually, she's basically shy."

Yes, she's basically shy and I'm basically poor, uneducated, and was raised in Alaska by a pair of polar bears.

"Shy?"

"That's right," her father said, "shy."

"You believe that?" Emma asked him in disbelief.

"Absolutely," Brent said. "She says that being with me helps bring her out of her shell."

Emma rolled her eyes. "Dad, I can't believe that you're this naive—"

"Emma, please," her father said quietly. "It's not like I was born yesterday."

"But your last girlfriend was—"

"Can I help it if I attract younger women?" her father said, a proud smile on his face.

"Dad, Princess got kicked out of boarding school for seducing the headmaster!"

I can't believe it—he's grinning again.

"Yes," her dad said, "she told me that story."

"And?"

"I understand she was sixteen and it was the other way around," her father said simply. "Anyway, it's in the past."

Emma took a deep breath. "Dad, I think she's wrong for you."

"Well, I think I'm past the age where I need my daughter's approval for my friends," Brent said, trying to hide his irritation with a jocular tone.

"It's not a matter of my approving or not—" Emma began.

"I brought her here to share a personal part of my life with you," Brent said. "Didn't we say we were going to communicate more?"

"Dad, bringing her here isn't exactly communicating—"

"I care for Princess very much," Brent said. "And you might as well know that we've been talking about marriage."

"Well, then, you have terrible taste," Emma said bluntly.

Brent Cresswell's eyes flashed fire and ice. He was a self-made millionaire many times over, and he wasn't used to insubordination—not even from his daughter.

"Why don't we just agree to disagree," Brent said in a cool tone. He picked up the menu. "Okay?"

Emma nodded.

Okay, I've said my piece. What else can I do? He's not ten years old and I am not his parent. But I can't believe he could think of this Princess person as a potential wife!

A white-jacketed waiter came, took their orders, and two big fresh green salads were placed almost immediately in front of them.

"Well," her father said to her again, "it's good to see you."

"It's been an exciting summer," Emma said in a stilted voice.

"Glad to hear it," Brent said. "When do you start school again?"

"September," Emma said coolly, "but I'm thinking about transferring."

Her father raised his eyebrows. "Transferring? Where? Your mother will have a heart attack if she hears that."

Emma smiled.

Dad may not have great taste in girlfriends, but he sure knows Kat.

"To a better school," Emma answered.

"My dear, Goucher is a fine school," her father said grandly. "Your mother went there. And her mother."

"Not for what I want," Emma stated matter-of-factly.

"You're changing majors?" her dad asked, taking a bite of salad.

"I haven't picked a major," Emma said honestly. "I do it this year."

"But I thought that French—"

"I like French," Emma said, "I really do."

"So?" her dad asked, confused.

"It's not what I want to major in," Emma said firmly.

This should throw him for a loop when I tell him what I'm interested in. I mean, he's never bothered to ask, Emma thought to herself with a grin.

"And what might that be?" Brent asked.

"Primate biology," Emma answered, as if she were reading an item off a shopping list.

"Well, Dr. Chanderot's one of the best in the world," her father said to her, totally nonplussed, "but he's in France."

Chanderot?! How does my father know about Dr. Chanderot, the guy I heard lecture in Portland last week!? That's completely impossible!

"How do you know about him?" Emma asked, astonished.

"*National Geographic* did a big story on him," her father explained. "And he came to Miami."

"What for?" Emma asked.

"To speak at the museum," Brent said. "I'm on the board."

"So," Emma ventured, "I was thinking about studying with him."

"Good," Brent said.

"Good?"

"Sure, why not?" her father said as he broke off a piece of bread.

"Because Mother will go crazy," Emma explained. "You said it yourself!"

"Oh, come on, Emma," Brent chided her. "What's a little insanity among family?"

"I just don't want—"

"Emma, you're a big girl," her father said gently. "Go where you want, study where you want. God knows you can afford it."

I can't believe he is totally supporting me on this, Emma thought. *That is the last thing that I expected. I might as well take the biggest plunge of all.*

"What would you think if I took a leave of absence from school and . . . joined the Peace Corps?" Emma asked.

Brent was silent for a moment. "The

Peace Corps?" he finally asked.

Emma nodded. "I'm trying to decide if I should study with Dr. Chanderot first, or just try to have the Peace Corps send me to Africa."

"Africa," Mr. Cresswell repeated.

"Right," Emma said.

"I have to admit, Emma, you are full of surprises," her father remarked.

"Not really," Emma replied. "I mean, this is something I've been thinking about for a long time. If we had ever spent any time together, you would already have known about it."

Brent inhaled quickly, registering the slight. "My opinion is, I would rather see you study in France than go traipsing off to the African wilds. However, I still maintain that you should do what you want to do."

Emma smiled at her father and began to feel genuinely good for the very first time since he'd arrived. "Thanks. I really appreciate that," she said sincerely.

"Look, if you want, I'll call your mother," Brent offered.

"But you don't talk to her!" Emma said, clearly surprised. "She told me that you two never speak!"

"She lied," Brent said.

"She did?"

"We still have a lot of business interests in common, Emma," her father explained. "You don't get divorced that easily these days."

"Oh," Emma said, noncommittally.

"Emma," her father said, reaching across the table for her hand. "I meant what I said. You should do what you really want to do. Don't let your mother, or me, or anybody hold you back! Life is too short!"

Emma felt a lump rising in her throat. She had been so sure that her father would voice a strong and vocal disapproval of her plans.

And although she was glad to have his support, it just illustrated how much they really didn't know each other at all.

SEVEN

Emma woke up early the morning after dinner with her father—it was Monday, the day that Jane and Jeff Hewitt usually went to the mainland to their law office, which meant that Emma had more work to do than usual.

She took a quick shower, dressed in a simple pair of white shorts and a pink cotton top, and went downstairs. To her surprise, Jane was sitting at the breakfast table, alone.

"Morning," Jane said cheerfully.

"Hi," Emma replied, heading for the teakettle. "I didn't expect to see you here. Where is everyone?"

"Jeff took Katie and Wills with him to the office," Jane said, sipping her morning coffee.

"That should be a treat," Emma said ironically, pouring herself a quick cup of tea.

"Can't start training those new lawyers too young!" Jane joked.

"What about Ethan?" Emma asked.

"He's been waiting for you to get up," Jane said. "He's out riding his bike. Ian Templeton invited him over this morning to swim."

Ian Templeton was rock superstar Graham Perry Templeton's thirteen-year-old son. Carrie worked for the Templetons as their au pair.

"Want me to take him?" Emma asked, sitting down with Jane.

"You got it," Jane said. "Take the BMW. I think Ethan's ready to roll."

Emma finished her tea, took the keys from Jane, ran upstairs to grab her sunglasses, and came back down to find Ethan waiting for her in the front hallway.

"Ian invited me over," he said happily, obviously impressed to be going to the home of one of the world's biggest rock stars.

"So your mom said," Emma noted, leading the way to the car.

"Lemme tell you something," Ethan said as he climbed in.

"What's that?" Emma asked.

"Ian's still kinda afraid to go out in public," Ethan said. "You know, because of *what happened.*"

"Because of what happened?" Emma queried, even though she knew perfectly well what Ethan was referring to. She turned the car down High Street and headed for the Templetons' house.

"You know, Emma," Ethan said confidentially. "*Rock On.*"

"Oh, *Rock On,*" Emma said, affecting Ethan's tone.

Emma knew that earlier in the summer, *Rock On* magazine had run a story about Ian that was a total hatchet job, and that had made fun of everything from Ian's small stature to his perceived status as rock icon Graham Perry's talentless son. Graham and his wife Claudia had filed suit, but it was still a major scandal on the island.

"All the kids have taken sides," Ethan said knowledgeably.

"Is that so?"

"A lot say Ian's a total goober," Ethan said, "but not me."

"Because of the article?" Emma queried.

Ethan nodded. "Other kids think it's really cool that he looked like he was smoking marijuana in that article," he added significantly.

"I know for a fact that story was completely fabricated," Emma said firmly.

"Maybe, maybe not," Ethan said knowingly. "Anyway, Ian is famous."

"Ethan, that story was all lies," Emma said. "And it is not at all cool for anyone to believe that Ian was smoking marijuana."

Ethan shrugged. "I didn't say I believe it."

Emma sighed and pulled the car up the Templetons' long driveway.

"Ian said to go around to the back, he'll be there," Ethan advised Emma.

Emma parked the Hewitts' car, then led Ethan through the gate to the built-in swimming pool the Templetons had installed at their house. Even though it was only nine-thirty in the morning, she could see Ian and his little sister, Chloe, splashing around, while Graham floated in the middle of the pool on a giant air raft, reading the sports section of *The Boston Sunday Globe*.

"Hey, Ethan!" Ian said happily when he saw Emma and Ethan come in. "Come on in!"

Ethan wasted no time. Emma watched him pull off his T-shirt, strip off his shoes, and do a gigantic cannonball leap into the pool. The water cascaded all over Graham's newspaper.

"Thanks, Ethan," Graham said mock-threateningly. "I needed that." But Emma could see he was smiling.

"Nice to see you, Emma," Graham called to Emma. "Carrie's inside—she'll be right out."

Emma nodded and sat down on one of the comfortable poolside chaise lounges. She took the book review section of the newspaper and started to read a long piece about African explorers.

She didn't hear Carrie sneak up behind her and toss a buttered bagel on the newspaper.

"Air mail," Carrie called. Emma looked up at her with a grin.

"Thanks," Emma said, picking up the

bagel. "I didn't eat yet."

"Then enjoy," Carrie responded, sitting down next to her friend. "How was dinner?"

"Dad or the food?" Emma queried.

"Dad," Carrie said.

Emma cocked her head and thought for a moment. "Okay, I guess," she said finally.

"You guess?" Carrie asked.

"With my family one can never be sure," Emma pronounced.

"Mine, too," Carrie added fervently.

"Mine, too!" Graham shouted to them, from the center of the pool.

The girls laughed, and then continued more quietly.

"We talked a lot about school, and the future, and that was okay," Emma said.

"Sounds good," Carrie acknowledged.

"But he's got a weird new girlfriend," Emma added.

"I know," Carrie said with a grin, "I met Princess."

"How?" Emma asked, surprised.

"Last night," Carrie said, "Billy and I were out on the boardwalk."

"So?" Emma asked. "What's that got to do with my dad's girlfriend?"

"Let me finish." Carrie grinned. "I went over to buy us a couple of ice cream cones, and when I came back to Billy there was this blond bimbo trying to pick him up."

"No way," Emma protested.

"No lie," Carrie insisted.

"So what'd you do?" Emma asked.

"Nothing," Carrie said with a shrug. "Billy wasn't interested."

"Hey," Emma said, "how did you know that the girl was Princess?"

"She gave Billy her comp card, and I saw a Miami address on it," Carrie explained. "And I heard her tell Billy that her 'old man' was having dinner with his daughter tonight."

Old man? She referred to my father as her old man? Emma thought distastefully. *Now that is really disgusting.*

"So you put two and two together—"

"You know how bright I am," Carrie teased.

"What a slut!" Emma exclaimed.

"I am not!" Carrie protested with a laugh.

"Very funny," Emma said, "you know I mean Princess-give-me-a-break-Alexis."

"She's a piece of work," Carrie agreed, reaching behind her for some sunblock.

"I told my father she was awful," Emma said. "He wouldn't listen."

"No one likes to hear that the person they're involved with is awful," Carrie pointed out.

"Well, sometimes the truth hurts," Emma said bluntly. "I refuse to keep my mouth shut about his little tramp—"

"Emma!" Claudia Templeton came to the back door of the house. "Phone! It's your father!"

"Good timing," Emma said with a sigh.

"Speaking of the devil," Carrie said. "Go get 'em."

How'd my dad get this number? Emma wondered as she made her way inside to the phone.

"Take it on the upstairs extension," Claudia Templeton told Emma.

Emma made her way up the stairs towards the kids' bedrooms and took the phone call up there.

"Hello?"

"Hi, Emma!" Brent said happily.

"Hi, Dad," Emma said. "I can't talk for long, I'm working."

"Working hard or hardly working?" her dad joked.

"Working hard," Emma said in a chilly voice.

"Hey, your old man is just teasing you," he assured her.

Emma winced when her father called himself her "old man." *God, that's how Princess refers to him. How very nauseating.*

"Listen, honey," Brent continued, "do you have plans for this afternoon?"

Emma thought a moment. *I have to take Ethan home for lunch, and then he has a swimming lesson, but after that I'm free.*

"I work till three," Emma said.

"What happens after then?" her father asked.

"I'm free until tonight," Emma replied.

"I'd love to see you again," Brent said to her. "I had such a great time last night."

"Me, too, Dad," Emma said without much enthusiasm.

"I've got a great idea," Brent suggested. "Why don't I make a tee-off time for three-thirty and you come out on the golf course with me?"

"Gee, Dad," Emma said, trying to keep her voice pleasant, "I hate golf!"

"You don't have to play," Brent enthused,

"just ride in the cart with me."

"Well . . . okay," Emma answered.

I really do want to talk to him again about his Princess. God knows what she'll be doing while we're out on the golf course.

"You need a ride to the club?" her father asked.

"I'll take the Hewitts' car," Emma said.

"Okay, three-thirty, see you there!" Brent said.

Golf, Emma thought. *With my father. I hope he doesn't actually expect me to take any swings. I'd rather watch paint dry than swing a golf club!*

Emma had walked past the golf clubhouse at the Sunset Country Club many times, but had never set foot inside. Until now. And as she walked in, all she could think was that even in her worst nightmare, there couldn't be so many rich people in the world dressed so incredibly badly as what she saw inside.

Pastel shirts. Plaid green trousers with yellow stripes. Knickers and black knee socks. Bright orange skirts with matching yellow-and-orange tops.

Keep Sam away from this place, Emma

thought to herself. *She'd have a fashion stroke. They'd have to carry her out of here!*

"Emma!"

Emma searched the room until she saw her father. He was standing near the door to the pro shop, and he had on one of those awful outfits, too—a lime-green shirt with a peculiar insignia on the chest, and black-and-green checked pants, with white golf shoes.

"Hi, Dad," she said, dubiously looking at his outfit.

"You don't like?" Brent asked, checking himself out in a nearby mirror. "I just bought the cap." He showed Emma a bright orange Sunset Country Club baseball-style cap that could not have gone worse with his clothes. Of course, he put it on.

"It's, well . . . colorful!" Emma managed, putting the best possible spin on things.

"We tee off in ten minutes," Brent said to her. "Our cart's waiting."

"*We* tee off?" Emma said skeptically. "No, *you* tee off."

"But all those golf lessons that summer—"

"When I was a child," Emma finished

his sentence for him, "are going to waste. Honestly, Dad, I didn't even much care for it then."

"You're missing out on a great sport," Brent told her.

"I'll risk it," Emma replied archly.

Ten minutes later Brent Cresswell was standing at the first tee of the golf course, with Emma ensconced behind the wheel of a roofed golf cart. She had a glass of iced tea sitting in a special holder on the cart, and a scorecard to use to keep score for her dad as he played.

"It's a beautiful day for golf," Brent sang out as he gently swung his driver from side to side. He looked down the fairway. The people playing in front of him had moved on. Then he stepped up to the tee, set up his white golf ball, and swung.

Whack! The ball fairly flew off the tee, and Emma could see it arcing lazily against the blue sky before dropping down the fairway, at least two hundred yards away.

Emma applauded.

Even I know a good shot when I see one.

"Thanks, hon," Brent said with a boyish grin on his face as he climbed into the cart, "but let's not get too enthusiastic."

"Why not?" Emma questioned nicely, starting to drive the electrically powered cart to where Brent Cresswell's ball lay.

"This is golf," Brent said with a grin. "You're as good as your last shot."

As if to prove himself correct, on his next swing, he banged the ball with his five-wood another two hundred yards, but this time he hit it right into a sand trap by the green that looked to Emma to be as wide as New Mexico.

"I see what you mean," Emma said as she drove the cart up to the trap. She could see that her dad's ball was buried almost halfway in the sand. Brent got out of the cart and scooted down into the bunker. He was practically hidden from Emma's view.

Emma decided not to bring up the subject of Princess until after her father had played the first hole. So she watched quietly as Brent blasted out of the trap onto the green, and then two-putted.

"Bogey," he said with a smile. "Mark it down."

Emma wrote the number "5" on the scorecard.

"Not a bad start," Brent said.

"For you," Emma added, then had to stop

and think why that had popped out of her mouth.

And then she remembered. A long ago summer, when she'd gone golfing with her father.

It was our joke, Emma recalled. *"Not a bad start," Daddy would say. "For you," I would reply. Oh, Daddy,* she wanted to cry out, *where did all the years go?*

"Yeah, kid, for me," her father agreed with a grin. He caught Emma's eye.

He's remembering, too! she realized.

"On to number two!" Brent called.

Emma drove to the tee for the second hole. *Maybe I should tell him about Princess and Billy now,* Emma thought. *I mean, we're starting to feel closer, and I'm sure he'll want to know the truth. . . .*

Okay. I'm not so sure. But I'm going to tell him, anyway.

And she did.

"So the thing is," Emma finished, "when Carrie came back, your Princess was practically draped all over Carrie's boyfriend!"

"She's just a warm, friendly, physical person," Emma's dad said with a shrug.

"Friendly?" Emma asked wryly. "Is that what you call it?"

"Look, Emma, she touches people a lot to compensate for her shyness!"

"Dad!" Emma cried, truly exasperated, "you don't actually believe that, do you?"

"I think this is a subject we should drop," Brent said easily. He got out of the cart, took an iron out of the cart, and hit his tee shot for the second hole.

"Decent," Brent said, returning to the cart.

"Dad?"

"What is it, honey?" Brent said.

"Tell me just one thing," Emma said, irritated by this whole situation with Princess.

"Anything," Brent said, studying the terrain for his next shot.

"Why are you with this girl?" Emma asked bluntly. "And why is she with you?"

Brent gave his daughter a hard look. "I like her, she likes me."

"I think she's after something," Emma responded.

"My money?" Brent asked. "I'm not stupid."

You're with her, Emma wanted to say, *which does not demonstrate the highest intelligence on your part,* but she held her tongue.

"Just watch out," Emma cautioned her father.

"Emma, honey, I know you mean well," her father said. "But I don't need nor do I desire your advice about my personal life." He lined up his shot and chipped to within ten feet of the cup.

"What a shot!" he yelled happily.

"You're as good as your last shot," Emma mumbled, her mind still on Princess.

"You're my lucky charm," her father said, clearly trying to improve her mood.

Emma smiled at him forlornly.

I wish . . . I wish . . . oh, why does it have to be like this? she thought miserably. *I know we could have some kind of a real relationship, so why doesn't it ever work out?*

Brent got out of the cart, went to the back of it, and took out his putter.

"Watch me sink this for a birdie," he called excitedly to his daughter.

"Good luck," Emma said, wanting somehow to find a common ground with him once again.

"Hey, I've got my beautiful daughter with me," Brent said, "it's a piece of cake."

Brent walked up to the flagstick that

was stuck in the cup and took it out. He laid it down on the green outside the range of his putt. He walked back on the green and lined up his putt carefully.

And then it happened.

Emma couldn't believe her eyes.

Brent Cresswell groaned and crumpled to the ground as if he had been punched in the stomach.

Emma ran to her father's side.

"Oh, my God! Oh, my God! Somebody please help!" Emma screamed.

"Emma," her father whispered. He grabbed his chest, clearly in horrible pain. "Help me, please."

"Where is everybody?" Emma screamed.

Her father was suffering a massive heart attack right in front of her and she had absolutely no idea what to do.

"Somebody please help!" she cried again.

EIGHT

Emma saw a golf cart rushing toward her. She waved frantically, then turned back to her father, prostrate on the ground. He kept whispering "help" in a tiny, raspy voice. A beetle starting to crawl up his head.

The cart ran right up on the green. Two men raced out of it toward her stricken father.

"Please help! I think he's having a heart attack!" Emma screamed.

A short man tossed a mobile phone to her.

"Call 911," he said. The other man was already working on her father, doing what Emma vaguely recognized as CPR.

I could have taken CPR at school, Emma thought dully. *But I didn't.*

Emma dialed 911.

"Portland Emergency," the female voice answered.

"This is Emma Cresswell," Emma said, trying to keep her voice steady. "My father is having a heart attack."

"Where are you?" the voice said.

"Sunset Island country club, on the golf course," Emma continued, "second green."

"Is there anyone with him?" the emergency operator asked.

"Yes, two men, one is giving him CPR."

"We'll send a med-evac unit, miss," the voice said. "Stay where you are."

The voice clicked off.

"There's a med-evac on the way," Emma said to the men working on her father.

"He's alive, miss," one of the men said. "Is he related to you?"

"My father," Emma answered, her voice cracking. "Please help him." She began to cry. "Can I hold his hand?"

"Stay out of the way," the larger man ordered gruffly as he continued to work on Emma's father.

Emma sat down on the green and put

her face in her hands.

As tears rolled down her cheeks, she began to pray.

More golf carts rolled up as people on the course saw that someone was in trouble.

In five minutes, that seemed to Emma like five hours, she looked up in the air at the sound of an airplane approaching. But it wasn't an airplane—it was a Bell Jet-Ranger helicopter painted with the markings of the Maine Medical Center.

It was the med-evac the 911 operator was talking about. Emma had had no idea what to expect.

The helicopter landed on the second fairway. As Emma watched, two uniformed paramedics climbed out carrying a stretcher, loaded her father into the helicopter, gave him an injection, and hooked him up to an EKG machine.

The man who had done the CPR ran over and talked quickly with the paramedics. Then he walked over to Emma.

"They want you over there," he said.

Emma nodded, trying to blink the tears out of her eyes. As she ran toward the helicopter a chant repeated itself over and over in her head.

God, please don't let my father die. Please, please don't let him die. "You're his daughter?" one of the paramedics asked.

"Yes," Emma managed to whisper.

"We're in touch with the hospital," the paramedic said to her, pointing to a telephone link attached to the EKG. "A doctor there can read the EKG."

"Okay," the second paramedic said into the phone. "They're telling us to move him. Let's go. Miss?" She motioned to Emma to climb into the helicopter. Emma did as she was told.

The helicopter lifted off the golf green. The last thing Emma remembered of the scene was the circle of golf carts swimming out of vision.

Two hours later Emma's father was in the intensive care unit at the Maine Medical Center in Portland, and Emma was slumped in a chair outside, looking as bad as she ever had in her life.

God, please don't let my father die. Please.

Just before they landed, the paramedics had waved a capsule of smelling salts under Emma's nose and she'd come to. Her father had been rushed out of the helicopter and into the hospital, straight to the intensive care unit. The doctors wouldn't let Emma in.

She had gone to the nearest pay phone, and in a daze dialed Kurt's number and told him what had happened and where she was. She asked him to call Jane. She felt as if she were watching herself doing this—as if she were only an observer at someone else's tragedy.

After that, she was responsible for doing all the emergency admissions paperwork for her father. People in white coats kept firing questions at her that she tried to answer as best she could.

But what do I know about my father's medical history? I barely even know my father.

That thought made her cry again. *Please, God. Don't let him die before I even get to know him.* She had never felt so completely, totally alone.

What if I'm responsible for this? What if he dies and it's all my fault? I'm the one who got him upset about Princess—why did I think I had to get involved with that in the first place? Oh, please, please don't let him die.

"Emma?"

Emma looked up at the sound of her name. Jane Hewitt was standing in front of her.

So was Kurt.

Emma picked herself up and threw herself into Kurt's arms, and cried like a baby.

"I'm so glad you're both here," she managed to say in between tears that streamed down and soaked her white tennis shirt.

"It's okay," Kurt said. "It's going to be okay. You did just fine."

"I did?" Emma mumbled. "I had no idea what to do, I was so scared. So scared."

"Emma, you did the right thing," Jane Hewitt said, looking down at her more like a mother than like her boss. "You got your father help and you're here with him now."

"I was so scared," Emma whispered, her heart still pounding in her chest as she clung to Kurt. "I was—I'm so scared."

"I know," Kurt said. "We all are."

"Who were those people who helped him?" Emma wondered.

"The paramedics?" Kurt asked.

"No," Emma said, "at the golf course—two men."

"I don't know," Kurt said, bewildered.

"Nobody said anything about anyone at the golf course."

"One of them gave him CPR," Emma said, "and the other had a mobile phone, but I don't know who they are."

"Miss Cresswell?" a male voice said to her.

Emma looked up. A handsome, slightly balding black man in a white coat was motioning to her.

"I'm Dr. Jones, chief cardiology resident at this hospital," he said as Emma walked toward him. "I'd like to speak with you a moment."

Emma left Kurt and Jane behind and walked into a small examining room with Dr. Jones.

"So far, so good," Dr. Jones said.

"Really?" Emma cried. "He's alive?"

"He's alive," Dr. Jones replied.

"Oh, thank you! Thank you!" Emma cried.

"Not so fast, Miss Cresswell," Dr. Jones cautioned her. "Your father's not out of the woods yet. He's had a major coronary infarction. The next twenty-four hours are crucial."

"You mean there's still a chance—"

"He could die?" Dr. Jones said. "Yes, I won't kid you. A very good chance."

"But there's also a chance—"

"He will live," Dr. Jones finished her sentence again. "My suggestion is that you call your family immediately. I've seen too many cases where people have waited, and then they're sorry. But your father is doing fairly well."

"He's . . . he's not that old," Emma said, "and he's healthy. I mean, he seems healthy . . ." She realized she was trying to talk the doctor into giving her a good prognosis for her father.

"We'll do everything we can," Dr. Jones assured Emma. "I'll be back shortly. Meanwhile, I assure you, he's in very good hands."

Emma walked slowly back to the waiting room. *He's alive, that's the important thing,* she told herself. She remembered that when he'd visited her on Paradise Island he'd been so tired one night that he'd canceled a dinner with her and her friends. *Has he been sick for a long time?* Emma wondered. *Have I been too caught up in my own life to even notice?*

"What did he say?" Kurt asked her as he

put his arm around her protectively.

"He said Daddy is alive and . . . he might live," Emma said softly. "He said I should call my family."

Call my family? What family? Kat?

"When can you go in and see him?" Jane asked Emma.

"I don't know," Emma replied. "He didn't say."

"Are you going to call your mother?" Jane asked quietly.

Emma put her hand to her head and rubbed her forehead anxiously. *But Mother hates Daddy.* "Should I?" she asked.

"I think so," Jane said.

"But my mother is so . . . she divorced him," Emma said, as if both Jane and Kurt didn't already know. "I don't believe she cares about him at all."

"It's your decision," Kurt said gently, "but if I were her, I'd want to know."

"Yes," Emma sighed, "I guess you're right. I'll call her."

"How about Princess?" Kurt asked.

"Are you kidding?" Emma responded bitterly. "She's not my family."

"I think you should call her," Kurt said, "it's the right thing to do."

"If you want to call her, *you* call her," Emma snapped, tears coming to her eyes again. "I have to go find my mother!" She wiped the back of her hand across her cheek to catch the tears and walked over to the pay phone in the corner.

Emma vaguely remembered that her mother was staying at the Sherry Netherland Hotel in New York City. She got the number from directory assistance in Manhattan, called the hotel, and asked for Austin Payne's suite.

"Just a moment," the hotel receptionist said. "I'll transfer you."

The phone rang four times before Kat Cresswell picked it up.

"Hello!" Kat said gaily.

"Mother?" Emma said tentatively.

"Emma!" Kat chirped. "How delightful of you to call, I've had just the most miserable day."

"Mother, there's a problem here—"

"Nonsense, Emma," Kat's loud voice sang animatedly through the phone, "nothing you've done today can compare to the day I've had. Picture this—I was shopping at Bergdorf Goodman—imagine me going for off-the-rack—but I was desperate—well, the saleswoman there was so rude I had to call the manager and tell her, and then there was a big to-do and they offered to pay for my lunch!"

"Dad's had a heart attack," Emma said quietly.

"Oh, Emma," Kat said with a laugh, "you just want me to be quiet and listen to you, so why don't you just say so?"

"Mother," Emma repeated, her voice growing steely. "Dad's in the intensive care unit. He had a heart attack out on the golf course this afternoon. He may die."

Emma heard nothing but silence for a moment.

"You're joking, of course," Kat said, her voice getting small and faraway.

"I am not joking," Emma said.

"So where is he? Where are you?" Kat asked. "In Florida?"

It occurred to Emma that her mother had no idea that her father had come up to visit her.

"Here in Portland, Mother," Emma said. "Dad came to Sunset Island for the weekend. He's at Maine Medical Center." Emma wiped one perspiring hand on the leg of her pants and bit her lip to keep herself from crying again.

"Oh," Kat breathed. "Oh, Lord . . ."

"Mother?"

"Yes, Emma?"

"I'm scared," Emma said, her voice breaking. "I'm more scared than I've ever been in my life!"

"Emma," Kat asked firmly, "what hospital did you say is treating him?"

"Maine Medical Center in Portland," Emma replied.

"And you're there?"

"Yes," Emma replied tonelessly. "In the lounge near the intensive care unit."

"I'll call you back," Kat said. She hung up.

Emma walked slowly back to Kurt and Jane Hewitt.

She's not going to call, Emma realized sadly. *She divorced him and she doesn't care. I'm going to have to handle this alone.*

"How'd it go?" Kurt asked.

"Awful," Emma admitted. "She said she'd call back but I know she basically doesn't give a damn."

"She may not care about your dad, Emma," Jane Hewitt said, "but I bet she gives a damn about you."

"You don't know my mother," Emma sighed.

"She's a mother," Jane said simply. "She cares."

"Then I wish she'd show it!" Emma sobbed onto Kurt's shoulder. "Why is this happening? I don't want my daddy to die!"

Kurt held Emma close in his arms for many minutes, until she was as cried out as she could be.

"I called Princess," Kurt said finally when Emma stopped sobbing.

Emma sniffled and took the Kleenex Jane handed her. "What did the Princess say?"

Kurt shrugged. "She said she'd be over soon."

"Ask me if I care," Emma said. "I hope she doesn't show up."

"It might mean a lot to your father," Jane said.

"Miss Cresswell?" Dr. Jones said, coming up next to Emma. "You can go in to see your father now."

"Is he—?" Emma asked, her face suffused with hope.

"He's awake," Dr. Jones said. "Don't be scared by all the medical equipment in there. Your father is comfortable—although he's pretty well out of it right now. Don't tire him."

"I won't," Emma promised.

Kurt gave her hand a squeeze and she walked to the intensive care unit. *I won't be scared,* she told herself. *I've seen intensive care units on TV. It'll be okay.*

Nothing she'd ever seen on television, however, quite prepared her for the sight of her father—strong, self-assured, dynamic, powerful Brent Cresswell, self-made millionaire, who'd never had anything worse than the common cold—hooked up to a life-support system.

He looks terrible, Emma thought, panic overtaking her. *He looks like he could die any minute.*

She squeezed her hands into tight fists, until her fingernails dug into her flesh so that the pain would keep her from crying.

I am going to be strong, Emma vowed. *I am not going to cry inside this room, no matter what I do, no matter what it takes, no matter how hard I cry when I leave here.*

She moved close to her father, who managed a wan smile. She took his hand in hers. "I'm here, Daddy," she said.

Then she felt the lightest touch on her hand as he squeezed her fingers in his.

Four hours later Brent Cresswell was still alive—doing still a little bit better, even, according to Dr. Jones. Dr. Jones had suggested that Emma go to the hospital cafeteria and try to eat something—there wasn't that much that Emma could do at intensive care except get more anxious, anyway.

Kurt led Emma down the escalator to the hospital cafeteria and through the food line. Emma didn't get anything more than a cup of tea. Jane had already left for home.

Emma and Kurt sat wearily at a table.

"You really should try to eat something, babe," Kurt said softly.

"I can't," Emma replied, blowing in her tea to cool it off.

"Emma?" a voice called from behind her.

Emma turned around to see Sam. And standing next to Sam was Carrie.

Without a word the three best friends put their arms around one another and held each other, while Emma cried all over again.

"Sorry, I can't seem to stop doing that," Emma said. "How'd you know where to find me?"

"A nurse at intensive care," Carrie told her. "We came as soon as we could. Jeff Hewitt called us."

"I'm so glad to see you," Emma said, sitting down with her friends.

"How's your dad?" Sam asked, a little fearfully.

"He's alive," Emma said.

"Not good, not bad," Kurt told them. "We'll know more soon."

"You must be scared to death," Carrie said as comfortingly as she could.

"I am," Emma said.

"Well, you don't have to go through it alone," Sam assured Emma. "We're right here with you."

"Thanks, Sam," Emma said, her lip trembling. "It's such a nightmare! I'm the one responsible for taking care of him, and I don't even know him!"

"What do you mean?" Carrie asked her.

"I mean the doctors are asking me this, and asking me that, and I don't know the answers," Emma said with exhaustion.

"So do the best you can," Sam suggested.

"I am," Emma said, "but what if it's not good enough? What if I mess up?"

"What you're doing for him now is the greatest gift any daughter could give . . ." Sam said. "You're there for him, Em."

Emma looked at Sam closely. She wasn't used to her friend Sam being so philosophical.

"And when he gets well," Sam continued, "he damn well better send you on the international shopping trip of all time!"

They all laughed, even Emma. The laughter broke the tension—at least part of it—for Emma.

"It's really great of you two to be here," Emma said fervently.

"Hey, what are friends for?" Sam replied.

"You know what the scariest thing is?" Emma asked. She stared into her cup of tea, then looked at Sam and Carrie. "The scariest thing is that I realized today that my parents are going to die."

"I know what you mean," Kurt said. "Even though I lost my mom, I still can't imagine my dad dying. It doesn't seem real."

Emma put her hand on Kurt's leg and looked into his eyes. *That's right,* she thought. *He's already lived through the death of a parent. He knows.*

Kurt put his hand over hers and gave her a warm smile of understanding.

She searched the faces of her three dearest friends in the world. "My dad doesn't really know me at all, you know," she said. "And I don't know him, either."

"Maybe you'll have a chance to change that," Carrie said compassionately.

"That's what I'm praying for," Emma told Carrie, tears coming to her eyes again. "I'm praying for just one more chance."

NINE

"Emma," Carrie said quietly, waking her friend up.

"Mmmmmm," Emma said, rousing herself out of her slumber.

Where am I? Emma thought dazedly, struggling to sit up. *It feels like my eyeballs have been screwed shut. It looks like a hospital. What am I doing in a hospital?* Then it all came back to her, and a wave of nausea overtook her. *My father—did he die?*

Emma snapped awake at this last thought.

"Why did you wake me?" she asked Carrie, clutching her friend's arm hard.

"Did my father die?"

"No, no," Carrie assured her quickly. "He's the same. No worse."

"Thank God," Emma said, rubbing the throbbing point just above her eyebrows. "How long was I asleep?"

"It's just past midnight," Carrie said, pointing to an institutional-looking wall clock.

"Oh," Emma replied dully.

"I've got to get back to the island," Carrie said. "The last ferry's leaving soon."

Emma nodded.

"But I called Graham and Claudia earlier," Carrie continued, "they're going to give me a lot of time off tomorrow."

"Thanks," Emma whispered.

"Sam left about an hour ago—she didn't want to wake you," Carrie explained. "She said to tell you that Dan Jacobs agreed to give her time off tomorrow, too."

"You mean later today, don't you?" Emma said, attempting a small smile. She ran her fingers through her dirty hair, pushing it off her face. Kurt had had a taxi shift that night, and had left only after making sure that Emma would not be alone at the hospital.

"Why don't you get a room, get some rest?" Carrie suggested.

"Because I've got to stay here!" Emma said anxiously. "What if something happens?"

"If, God forbid, something happens," Carrie explained, "they'll call you. They told me at the nursing station there's a Ramada Inn across the street."

"No, I can't," Emma said. "If I'm here he—he can't die! But if I leave . . ." She let the rest of her sentence trail off.

"I don't think that's how it works," Carrie said gently. "And you'll do your dad much more good if you're rested so you can think clearly."

She's probably right, Emma thought to herself. *There's not a lot of good I can do here, now. I'll come back early in the morning. And if there's anything I have to make a decision about, I'll be fresh. Well, fresher, anyway.*

"Come on, I'll walk you over there," Carrie coaxed.

"Okay," Emma finally agreed, standing up. "Let me tell them at the nurses station where I'll be."

"I already did," Carrie told Emma. "I told them I was going to take you over there—

they have everything they need."

"Thanks, Carrie," Emma said sincerely. "You're a great friend."

"Hey," Carrie replied honestly, "that's what I'm here for."

"I guess that's right," Emma said quietly as the two girls walked through the deserted corridors of the hospital.

"Oh, one more thing," Carrie said, reaching into the small nylon backpack she was carrying and pulling out a plastic bag.

"What's this?" Emma asked, taking the bag from Carrie.

"Some stuff for you that Jane forgot to give you earlier," Carrie said. "Clothes, toothbrush, things like that."

"That was so thoughtful of her."

"She figured you'd need them," Carrie explained.

"She figured right," Emma sighed.

Emma left word at the front desk of the motel to wake her at eight in the morning, and to immediately put through any call that came from the hospital. She took a shower and got into bed, though she truly doubted that she'd be able to sleep even for a minute. But she closed her eyes and tried to at least nap.

BRRRING!

Emma woke up with a start and reached for the phone in a panic, her heart pounding.

"This is your wake-up call," a computerized voice said. "Good morning!!"

Emma hung up the phone and fell back on the bed. She had fallen asleep almost instantly, and it was morning already.

My heart's racing a million miles a minute, she thought to herself. *I thought that something had happened to Dad. Something worse.*

She washed up and then dressed hurriedly in a pair of jeans and a cotton print shirt from the bag Jane had sent, brushed her hair quickly, and ran out through the hotel lobby toward the hospital without putting on any makeup.

"Are you checking out?" the perky motel desk clerk asked as Emma ran past the front desk.

"Not today," Emma replied, on the run.

She rushed over to the hospital and up to the intensive care unit nursing station.

"I'm Emma Cresswell," she said, stopping in front of the nursing station. "My father is Brent Cresswell. In there." She pointed to the intensive care unit.

The nurse looked down at her papers and took out a file that said CRESSWELL on the outside.

"How is he?" Emma insisted, her voice rising.

The nurse looked up at her. "He seems to be resting comfortably," she said. "Dr. Jones is already in. Why don't you have a seat?"

"Can I see my father?" Emma said.

"He's asleep," the nurse replied.

Emma walked over to the door leading into the ICU and looked in. Sure enough, there was her father, tubes everywhere, hooked up to a heart monitor, fast asleep.

It might be my imagination but it looks like he has a little better color today, Emma thought.

"Good morning, Miss Cresswell," said Dr. Jones from behind her.

"Good morning," Emma said. "How is he?"

"The same, basically," Dr. Jones said. "Maybe a touch better. His heart rate is steady, and that's good."

"That's good?" Emma repeated, anxious for any good news.

"Yes," Dr. Jones said. "That's good. His blood pressure dropped a bit last night, but that's nothing to worry about."

"Are you sure?" Emma asked, clenching and unclenching her hands anxiously.

"Everything is under control," Dr. Jones assured her.

"Good," Emma murmured, not feeling any less anxious.

"You can go in and see him." Dr. Jones pointed to a computerized ICU digital display by the nursing station, which showed each ICU patient's heart rate, temperature, blood pressure, and some other information that Emma couldn't figure out. "It looks like he's waking up."

"Thank you," Emma said, and she hurried into the ICU, to her dad's bedside.

"Dad?" she said quietly.

Her father turned his head weakly in her direction.

"Mother," he said, just as weakly.

"No," Emma said, feeling sick inside. "It's me, Emma."

"Mother," Brent repeated, looking at Emma closely.

"It's me, Dad," Emma repeated. She gulped hard. "Emma. Your daughter."

"What?" her father mumbled.

"Emma," she said again. "How do you feel?" She reached for his hand.

"Mother, I don't want to go," Emma heard her father whisper. "I'm not going."

Dr. Jones came up behind Emma. She turned to him quickly, tears in her eyes.

"He thinks I'm his mother," she managed to blurt out.

"It happens sometimes," Dr. Jones said gently, looking at the monitors above Emma's father. "It's not a problem now."

Not a problem now, Emma mused anxiously. *That means it can be a problem later.*

"Can he hear me?" Emma asked the doctor.

"I honestly don't know," Dr. Jones said.

"When is he going to be normal?" Emma asked, biting her lower lip fearfully.

"Usually, if they're confused like this, it takes a day or two," Dr. Jones said.

"But he will be normal again," Emma said. "Won't he?"

"It's probably just temporary," Dr. Jones said.

Probably. Not for sure.

She turned back to her father. "Dad," she

said quietly, "I'll be here with you all the way. Don't worry, everything's going to be fine. You're in good hands."

She had no idea whether her father could understand her or not.

Emma left the ICU blinded by the tears she wouldn't allow herself to shed while visiting her father. She rounded the corner, heading for the ladies' room, and almost ran into a beautiful, chic, well-dressed woman.

It was her mother.

"Mother?" Emma whispered. "You're *here*?"

"Yes, clearly I'm here," Kat Cresswell said. She led her daughter over to some chairs.

Emma just stared at her mother, overcome. "You're actually here," she repeated.

Kat straightened her back and folded her hands in her lap. "Yes," she said.

Why, she's been crying, Emma realized, looking at her mother's red-rimmed eyes.

"What are you doing here?" Emma asked in a daze.

"Didn't you get my message?" Kat asked.

"What message?" Emma asked, mystified.

"I told you last night that I'd call you back!"

"I didn't get any message!" Emma exclaimed.

"Well, I talked to them," Kat said with some of her usual superciliousness, pointing to the ICU nursing unit. "They told me they'd tell you I called and that I was coming."

"Why are you here?" Emma asked her mother again, some of her old anger and resentment at Kat welling up inside her.

"What do you take me for?" Kat said to Emma, getting angry herself. "A witch?"

"No," Emma said defensively, "but—"

"Your father's just had a heart attack," Kat said in a controlled voice. "You're my daughter. I'm here."

"Where's Austin?" Emma asked.

"In New York," Kat responded. "Where else would he be?"

"Here with you," Emma answered.

"He's not my husband," Kat said quickly.

This is so odd, Emma thought. *I never would have thought that my mother would come here. I thought she didn't give a damn about my father and that she was too self-*

centered to care about me. But here she is.

"I'm glad you're here," Emma admitted, her voice trembling.

Kat reached for Emma's hand and held it tightly for a moment. "Can I see him?" Kat asked Emma.

Emma thought quickly. *I know my mother. If she sees my father in this condition she'll totally freak out. If she freaks out I'll freak out. No way.*

"Uh, he can only have one visitor an hour," Emma said, making it up as she went along.

"So?" Kat asked.

"So I was just in there," Emma finished.

"How is he?" Kat asked insistently.

Emma caught sight of Dr. Jones hurrying by and she called to him. "This is my mother, Katerina Cresswell," Emma said, introducing her mother to Dr. Jones.

The doctor shook Kat's hand. "Your husband is doing as well as can be expected," Dr. Jones said.

"Thank you," Kat said.

Emma gave her a quick look. *She didn't even bother to correct the doctor when he referred to Daddy as her husband!* Emma thought.

"Dr. Jones," Kat said in her most regal voice, "could you introduce me to the chief resident?"

"I *am* the chief resident," Dr. Jones replied.

"Well, do you mind telling me where you went to medical school?" Kat continued, her eyebrows raised in question.

Oh, God, my mother is doing this because Dr. Jones is black, it occurred to Emma with embarrassment.

Dr. Jones looked at Kat with a wry smile on his face. "A very good medical school," he responded solemnly.

"Which one?" Kat pressed. "Someplace offshore?"

"Yes, Mrs. Cresswell," Dr. Jones said pointedly. "Someplace offshore. Someplace called Harvard."

"Oh!" Kat brightened. "You were joking with me."

"Mrs. Cresswell," Dr. Jones said quietly, "my training is not a laughing matter. Excuse me." He went back into the ICU to tend to Brent Cresswell and the other patients on the critical list.

* * *

After lunch with her mother in the hospital cafeteria Emma and Kat went back to the ICU. There was a message waiting there for Emma that Carrie and Sam would be over to visit in the midafternoon. The nurse also told Emma that it would be okay if she wanted to go in and see her dad.

"Mother," Emma said to Kat, "wait here." She pointed to the ICU waiting room.

"But, Emma, I want to—"

"Please," Emma said, cutting her off. "Just sit down and wait."

Kat clamped her mouth shut. Then, like a little child, she meekly did as she was told.

Emma walked into the ICU, to her father's bed. He was awake, staring at the ceiling.

I am not going to cry, no matter what happens!

"Dad?" Emma said to him quietly.

Brent Cresswell turned and looked at his daughter.

"Emma," he croaked.

He recognized me. Thank God.

"Dad," Emma said, mustering as much courage as she could, "you're going to be fine, that's what the doctor told me."

"I've had a heart attack," her father said.

"Yes," Emma said, "but you're so much—"

"Christ," Brent whispered. "Other people get heart attacks. Not me. God, I'm sorry, Emma."

"Don't be sorry," Emma said. "Just get well."

Her father nodded weakly.

"Where's Princess?" he asked Emma in his paper-thin voice.

"Princess?" Emma asked, buying a little time. *I forgot all about her,* Emma realized. *I have no idea where she is or what she's doing, and I couldn't care less.*

"You called her?" Brent asked weakly.

"She was called," Emma hedged, since it was actually Kurt who had done the calling.

"As soon as she gets here, send her in," Brent whispered.

"Okay, Dad," Emma agreed.

Brent closed his eyes. "I'm not sleeping," he mumbled. "I'm resting. Don't go."

Do I tell him about Kat being here? Emma wondered anxiously. *I better, she might just barge in otherwise. I can only fend her off for so long.*

"Uh, Daddy?" Emma asked.

"Yes?" he whispered weakly, not opening his eyes.

"Mother's here," Emma said. "I called her last night and she came up from New York."

"Kat?" He opened his eyes and stared at Emma. "Kat is here?"

"Do you want to see her?" Emma asked her father.

He was silent for a moment, staring into the distance. "My wife," he finally whispered.

"Your ex-wife," Emma reminded him gently.

Brent gave Emma the tiniest of smiles. "My ex-wife," he agreed. He clutched Emma's hand hard. "Tell me the truth—do I look like a gray old man?"

"No, of course not—" Emma protested.

He grabbed her hand harder. "The truth," he rasped.

"You look sick," Emma said gently.

"Not old?" Brent Cresswell pressed.

"No, Daddy," Emma said. "Not old."

The corners of his mouth went up minutely. "In that case, Emma . . . send her in."

TEN

"He wants to see you," Emma told her mother.

"He does?" Kat asked incredulously.

"That's what he said," Emma responded.

Kat still sat there.

"I don't want to go in alone," Kat said finally. She put on her little girl voice. "Will you come in with me?"

Emma sighed. It was so difficult to follow her mother's mood swings—at one moment imperious, the next childlike and dependent. "Sure," Emma replied, "if they'll let me." She went over to the nursing station and talked quickly with the head nurse, who gave Emma permission to go in with her mother for five minutes, not a moment more.

Emma walked back to her mother. "Let's go."

Kat stood up, a look of panic on her face. "Wait! How do I look?"

"Impeccable," Emma replied evenly, trying to control her temper.

"I know that," Kat said testily. "I mean do I look . . . older than thirty-five?"

Emma closed her eyes and prayed for strength. "Mother, I don't really care how old you look right now," she said, gritting her teeth. "This is not about you!"

Kat smiled a sad smile. "Emma, dear, I know that. I want to look young for your father."

"He doesn't care—" Emma began.

"Oh, yes he does," Kat corrected her daughter. "You see, if I look young, then that means he is still young. If I look old, then he must be old."

Emma stared at her blankly.

"You'll understand one day," Kat said, running her hands over her skirt to smooth the watered silk fabric. "Let's go."

They went into the ICU, past four or

five other patients on the critical list, and headed over to Brent's bed. He lay there, resting, his eyes closed.

"Brent Cresswell, how could you?" Kat mock-chided her ex-husband. "How dare you have a heart attack before you sink your putt!"

Brent Cresswell looked up at his ex-wife.

And then he smiled.

"I got excited," Brent said weakly.

"Ha, fine golfer you turned out to be," Kat said, bending over to kiss her ex-husband on the forehead.

"Do us all a favor, Brent," Kat said, sitting down in the chair closest to his bed.

"What's that, Kat?"

"Don't go making any holes in one!" Kat joked, a regal look on her face.

Emma's father almost sort of managed a weak laugh. "I don't think you need to worry too much about that," he whispered. "At least not today."

This is unbelievable, Emma thought. *My mother, who told me that my father never speaks to her, and my father, who told me that he does speak to her but only about business, are joking around like an old married couple. I can't remember them teasing each other like this when they were actually married to each other!*

"I called Dr. Aubrey Smythe, that famous heart specialist we met in Telluride on that god-awful ski trip years ago, remember? He's related to the Popes."

Brent nodded.

"He told me you're in excellent hands with Dr. Jones, and he's planning to call here to check on your condition," Kat added.

"Thanks," Brent said softly.

"Well, what are ex-wives for?" Kat said, shaking her blond hair off her face.

"You look . . . wonderful," Brent said.

"I need to lose five pounds," Kat said, "but I'll do." She leaned close to his bed and gently pushed his hair off his forehead. "You need a haircut," she said softly.

"Yeah," he murmured, his eyes closing.

"Actually it looks kind of dashing long in the front like that," Kat added.

Brent Cresswell smiled but didn't open his eyes.

I can't believe it. She's flirting with him, Emma marveled.

A white-coated nurse came into the room. "You're going to have to leave now," she said to Emma and her mother, "Dr. Jones needs to see Mr. Cresswell."

She started ushering Emma and Kat out of the room.

Kat turned to her ex-husband as she was leaving. "I might let you take me to dinner when you get out of here," she said. "But do get some color first, Brent."

Emma saw the smile on her father's face as she and her mother walked out of the ICU.

"You were great with him," Emma admitted.

"I should be," Kat replied, taking a seat in the waiting area. "I've known him forever."

"Did you really call this Dr. Smythe?" Emma wondered.

"Absolutely I did," Kat confirmed.

"Why?" Emma asked pointedly, remembering how her mother had treated Dr. Jones. "Because Dr. Jones is black?"

Kat shook her head. "No, though I realize that's what you thought. Actually, I couldn't care less if Dr. Jones were green, all I care about is how qualified he is, because he is taking care of your father."

"I had no idea you even cared . . ." Emma murmured.

"Well, let this be a lesson to you," Kat said imperiously. "Someday you might have to do the same thing for me."

"You're actually eating!" Carrie approved as Emma took a small bite of her chicken sandwich.

"I am," Emma agreed. It was sunset. When Carrie and Sam arrived they'd coaxed Emma into going back over to the Ramada Inn's restaurant for some food.

"What's going on with your mother?" Sam asked as she poured ketchup all over her french fries. She and Carrie had seen Kat through the glass door of the ICU, sitting by Emma's father's bed.

"She won't leave him," Emma said matter-of-factly.

"Too weird," Sam opined, reaching for her Coke.

"You're telling me," Emma agreed.

"I thought they hated each other," Carrie said.

"So did I," Emma said. "It's just so strange. But she's so good with him—he actually smiles for her! And she flirts with him!"

"Where's Princess?" Sam asked. "Out giving her comp cards to the marines?"

"I haven't heard from her and she hasn't shown up at the hospital," Emma said, "so who knows."

"Wow, that really sucks," Sam said. "I mean, when you have a relationship with someone, you like to think that they'll be there for the rough stuff, you know?"

Emma nodded. *My mother, who professed to despise my father, is the one who is actually there for the rough stuff,* she realized. *Life is just so strange.*

"Well, speaking of the kind of person who sticks around," Carrie began, "is Kurt coming back tonight?"

"Did I hear my name?" a male voice asked.

Emma turned around and there was Kurt. She stood up and wrapped her arms around his neck. He held her silently for a moment. "I'm so glad to see you," she murmured.

"Your mom told me you were over here," Kurt told her. He held her at arm's length and studied her face with concern, pushing some hair off her face. "You look beat."

"I'm okay," Emma assured him. They sat

back down with Carrie and Sam. "Want to order something?"

"No, I ate," Kurt said. "I was really surprised to see your mom over there."

"She won't leave him," Sam told Kurt with a shrug. "Weird, huh?"

"Sometimes it takes a crisis to realize just how much someone means to you," Kurt said, looking at Emma significantly.

She reached over and took his hand gratefully. *I know just what he means,* she thought. *Just exactly what he means.*

"You sure you want me to go in with you?" Kurt asked Emma an hour later. They were standing outside the door to the ICU.

"Yes," Emma replied.

Her mother caught Emma's eye through the glass and came out of the ICU.

"How's Dad?" Emma asked.

"A little better, I think," her mother said. "Well enough to be getting annoyed with me. That's a good sign."

"I will never understand the two of you," Emma told her mother.

"That's fine, dear," Kat said. "No one expects you to."

Brent's face lit up when he saw his

daughter. His bed was cranked forward and he was sitting up.

"You look better!" Emma said happily.

"Hey, can't keep this old horse down," her father said. His voice still sounded weak, but not as trembly as it had before. "Hello there, young man," Brent added.

"Hello, sir," Kurt said politely. "How are you?"

"I've been better," Emma's father said. "But my daughter's been taking really good care of me." He smiled fondly at Emma.

"I love you, Daddy," Emma whispered.

"And I love you," her father replied. "Listen, I didn't want to ask this when your mother was around," Brent continued. "Have you heard from Princess?"

Emma looked at Kurt, but it was too late.

"I called her," Kurt said, "and—"

"And she's . . . got some kind of a bug," Emma quickly finished Kurt's sentence. "She . . . she can't get out of bed."

Kurt looked at Emma curiously but she kept a straight face.

"Poor kid," Brent commiserated. "Well, I'm sure she'll be here tomorrow."

"I'm sure," Emma heard herself saying.

Okay, tomorrow we'll tell my father the truth about Princess. Actually, tomorrow I'll talk to Dr. Jones about telling my father the truth about Princess. He's going to get upset. Really upset.

"Sorry to kick you two out," Brent said, "but I'm a little tired now."

"I'll be back as soon as you're awake," Emma promised, kissing her dad on the forehead.

"You take care of my girl, now," Brent mumbled, already half asleep. "She's precious, you know."

Kurt looked over at Emma. "I know that, sir," he said solemnly. "I'll never forget that, not as long as I live."

Brent Cresswell fell asleep with a smile on his face.

ELEVEN

"Hi, Daddy," Emma said, crossing the room to kiss her father. She tossed a copy of *The Boston Globe* onto his lap. "You look better!"

It was the next morning, and Emma was feeling better. Dr. Jones had just told her that her father was going to be moved to a private room later that day. He'd also given her advice on how to handle telling her father the truth about Princess.

"I am better," her father said in a much more vigorous voice than the day before. He scanned the front page of the paper. "Huh, the Red Sox lost again." He looked up at his daughter. "Dr. Jones is springing me soon."

"To a private room, you mean," Emma said, taking a seat by her father's bed. "I know. He just told me."

"Where's your mother?"

"Still asleep," Emma replied. "The Do Not Disturb sign was still up when I walked by her room."

Brent smiled. "The thought of your mother staying in a Ramada Inn is hilarious." He drummed his fingers on the newspaper. "It's just as well Princess has been sick—it would have been awkward to have her visit while your mother was here."

Emma took a deep breath. "Uh, Dad?"

Her father looked at her expectantly.

"There's something about Princess I have to tell you," Emma continued hesitantly.

"So, tell me," her father said. He sipped from his cup of decaffeinated tea.

"She's . . . not coming to the hospital," Emma said.

"Of course she is," Brent replied. "As soon as she's better. Today, I hope," her father replied.

"No, Dad," Emma said, feeling a little sick herself, "she's not coming."

"That's absurd, Emma."

"Dad," Emma said hesitantly, "I didn't want to have to tell you this. I . . . I lied about Princess being sick." Emma looked closely at her father to gauge his reaction. *Dr. Jones said it was okay to tell him the truth,* Emma reminded herself. *He said to be honest, but kind and understanding. Am I being kind and understanding?*

"You lied?" her father repeated with a frown.

"Yes," Emma said. "Princess left the island."

Brent blanched and put down his tea. "Where is she?"

"I'm not sure," Emma admitted. "I think she went back to Florida."

"She just . . . left?" Brent asked dully.

"I'm sorry, Dad," Emma said. "The truth is . . . well—I never talked to her. Kurt called her the night you got sick and told her you were here and she said she was coming, but she never showed up."

Emma saw her father sink lower into his pillows, a look of shame and humiliation on his face.

"I'm sorry, Dad. I really am," Emma said as comfortingly as she could.

"No, you're not," Brent said. "You actually think I'm getting exactly what I deserve."

"I know you really care for her," Emma said quietly.

Brent Cresswell looked down at his newspaper to avoid Emma's eyes. "I did," he admitted in a low voice. "You must think your father is a fool."

"No—" Emma protested.

"Oh, yes," her father said. "And I am a fool. An old fool."

"You're not old!" Emma insisted.

"I feel old," Brent said. "Used up and old."

Emma couldn't think of what to say. How could her strong, dynamic father feel old and used up? *It's too scary!* Emma thought. *This isn't Daddy!*

"It's strange, isn't it?" Brent said, an ironic smile on his lips. "My girlfriend went away when I needed her, but your mother came here."

"A little," Emma agreed.

"A lot," her father murmured. It looked to Emma like he was getting very tired.

"Emma," her dad asked, "please do one thing for me."

"Anything," Emma said sincerely.

"Don't mention Princess to your mother," Brent said, looking right at Emma. "Please."

"Okay," Emma said.

She'll find out anyway, she thought. *Kat always finds out.*

"I'm sure she'll find out about Princess eventually," Brent said, as if he could read Emma's mind. "But not right away."

"Dad, are you okay about this?" Emma asked, concern etched on her face.

"I don't have a whole hell of a lot of choice, do I?" he asked gruffly.

"I guess not," Emma agreed.

Her father smiled tiredly and scratched at the graying beard coming in on his face. "On the other hand, nothing focuses the mind on what's important like a good coronary."

"Emma! Hey, Emma! Wake up!"

Emma opened her eyes, and saw Ethan Hewitt's smiling face at her bedroom door.

"Hi, Ethan," Emma said, somewhat groggily. "What time is it?"

"Eleven o'clock," Ethan reported. "Mom said I should wake you."

"Thanks," Emma said, rubbing her eyes. *Better get up,* she realized. *I'm supposed to meet Kat for lunch at noon.*

"I'll go make you tea," Ethan offered, and he disappeared.

Emma got up and stretched out deliciously, and went to look out her window. The sun was shining in brightly, and she could see a small flotilla of monarch butterflies sailing along on the wind.

Nice day, she thought. *Really nice. And I can't remember the last time I truly appreciated the simple beauty of a day.*

It was three days after her father had been moved out of intensive care into his private room, and every day Dr. Jones reported that he was getting stronger and stronger. Brent Cresswell wouldn't have to be in the hospital for much longer, although Dr. Jones did lecture Emma several times on how much he would have to change his life-style in order to protect his health.

The Hewitts had been wonderful about everything. They had given her as much time off as she needed, encouraging her to spend time with both of her parents. In fact, she'd checked out of the Ramada Inn just the day before, arriving back at the Hewitts' house after the kids were already in bed. Jeff and Jane had stayed up talking with her—Emma was reminded once again that they were the greatest employers in the world.

Astonishingly, Kat had absolutely refused to go back to New York so long as Brent was in the hospital.

"If he's there," she'd said defiantly two days ago, "I'm here." There was no point in arguing with Kat, that much Emma knew from experience.

Emma showered and dressed quickly, putting on a Goucher College sweatshirt and jeans, and went downstairs.

Little Katie Hewitt screamed with joy when she saw Emma and jumped into Emma's arms.

"Emma, we missed you!" Katie sang out.

"I missed you, too," Emma replied, hugging the little girl.

"When can you take me to the pool?" Katie begged her. "Soon?"

Emma smiled. "Soon, I hope."

Then Wills came over, a little sheepishly, and Emma scooped him up, too, and gave him a big hug.

"I'm glad your father's okay," he said, trying to sound as grown-up as possible.

"Me, too!" Emma said fervently.

"Here's your tea, Emma!" Ethan said, putting a full teakettle on the table.

"Thanks, Ethan," Emma said gratefully, sitting down at the breakfast table, where Jane Hewitt regarded the whole group proudly.

"That's the full Hewitt honor guard greeting," she said, "reserved only for very special occasions."

"I'm honored," Emma said, a lump forming in her throat.

Could life actually be getting back to normal? It looks pretty normal around here, Emma thought happily.

"Your mother called," Jane reported. "Everything's fine at the hospital and she'll meet you at noon."

Emma looked at her teacup, and at the teapot. It all seemed so normal to her, it was hard to believe that a few days earlier her father had nearly dropped dead on the golf course.

"It's so good to be back here," Emma said shyly.

"It's good to have you back," Jane Hewitt said. "Now, let's work on getting your dad out of that stupid hospital so that you can get back to work!"

"Amen!" Emma said, and everybody laughed.

Emma sat across from her mother at their luncheon table on the deck of the Sunset Inn and looked past her out at the ocean. They had just ordered seafood salads and iced tea.

It all seems so clear, so beautiful now, she thought. *And I take it for granted so often! I am so lucky to be young and healthy and alive!*

"That's quite an outfit you have on," Kat said, looking with disapproval at Emma's sweatshirt and jeans.

"This?" Emma asked, looking down at herself. She grinned. *A week ago that remark would have upset me,* Emma thought. *And today I realize that it just doesn't matter. It really doesn't matter!*

"No problem," Emma said breezily. "You don't have to wear it. You're looking nice, though."

Kat had on an extremely tasteful blue silk shirt tucked into a white calf-length silk skirt, and a pair of blue espadrille shoes. The whole ensemble was topped off by a magnificent straw hat trimmed in blue, and a pair of designer sunglasses from Paris.

"Thank you," Kat replied, clearly disgruntled that she hadn't gotten the slightest rise out of her daughter. "You know, there's no reason for you to dress commonly just because other girls your age do," Kat continued, unwilling to let the subject go.

Emma picked up a breadstick and took a bite, not rising to her mother's bait.

"I just hate to see you letting yourself go—" Kat groused. "No makeup, a sweatshirt, a pair of old—"

"Hi, there!" a friendly male voice called.

Emma turned around to see Kurt's grinning face.

"Hi!" Emma cried, jumping up to hug her boyfriend. "What are you doing here?"

"Picking up a fare, actually," Kurt said easily. "I'm doing a double shift on the taxi today—one of the guys is sick," he explained. "I saw you from the lobby."

"Can you come back and join us?" Emma asked hopefully.

"Sorry, gotta work," Kurt said. He turned around to scan the lobby just as a middle-aged man in tennis shorts strode to the front desk. "That must be my guy," Kurt said. "He told me he'd be dressed for tennis. Gotta run. Bye!" Kurt kissed Emma on the cheek and sprinted for the lobby.

"He could have acknowledged me at least," Kat said, fluffing her hair.

"He was working," Emma explained. "Usually he's very polite."

"Your salads," the waitress said, setting two huge, beautiful salad bowls in front of them. "Can I get you anything else?"

"Not at the moment," Kat said. She picked up her fork and began to eat her salad. "Mmmm, lovely," she commented. "Your boyfriend is very hardworking, isn't he?"

"Yes," Emma replied, eating some salad.

"He isn't like any of your other boyfriends," Kat pointed out.

"He's wonderful," Emma said simply.

"He's . . . disadvantaged, isn't he?" Kat said delicately.

Emma put down her fork. "What is that supposed to mean?"

"I mean he's poor, Emma. It's not his fault, it's just the way it is," Kat explained.

"Well, he won't be poor forever," Emma said, heat coming to her face. "And he's not poor in any of the ways that are really important." She clenched her fists under the table. *How can she be getting to me, after everything we've both been through? After all my vows that things would be different—*

"Lovely words, dear," Kat said. "But did it ever occur to you that he's, well . . . after something?"

Emma felt the seafood she'd eaten turn over in her stomach. *That's exactly what I told Dad about Princess,* Emma realized. *But Kurt is nothing like that! Kurt loves me!* "He is after something, Mother," Emma replied, trying to control her voice. "He loves me and he wants to marry me. That's what he's after!"

"He wants to marry you?" Kat asked, aghast. "But I'm not old enough to have a married daughter!"

"Mother, this doesn't have anything to do with you!" Emma yelled. A silver-haired man at the next table gave her a look of disapproval. Emma took a deep breath. "Look, Mother, I'm not getting married right now, okay? I love Kurt and Kurt loves me. Now, let's just drop the subject."

They ate in silence for a few minutes.

"Emma, do you find it odd that I'm here?"

Kat asked her daughter.

"Yes," Emma said bluntly. "I never even expected you to show up."

"When you called me the night Brent got sick," Kat said truthfully, "I had no intention of coming."

"Because you hate Dad," Emma suggested.

"Because of a lot of things," Kat said. "For one, Austin did not want me to come up here."

"Austin!" Emma said. "He doesn't run your life!"

"He's the man I live with," Kat said simply.

"But it's your decision," Emma insisted.

"That's what I decided," Kat said, agreeing with her daughter. "Eventually."

"So you came because of me?" Emma asked.

"Yes," Kat agreed. "But I stayed because of Brent."

"Meaning?" Emma asked.

"You obviously can handle everything now, Emma," Kat said. "You've proved that to everyone."

"So why don't you go," Emma said, "if you want to?"

"That's the thing," Kat said, talking as honestly as Emma could remember. "Every time I call my travel agent to book a flight I hang up the phone."

"So you don't really want to leave," Emma tried to understand her mother's feelings.

"Evidently not," Kat said. "But I can't tell you why. I mean, I'm not ready to remarry your father."

"Who said anything about remarriage?"

"No one," Kat said.

"You just did," Emma pointed out. "You said you're not ready to remarry Dad."

"Did I?" Kat asked in her gay, little girl voice. "Now wouldn't that be hilarious! Do you think he still wants me?"

"I haven't any idea," Emma answered, feeling dizzy. *Is my mother actually sitting here asking me if my father still wants her?*

"I suppose I just want to know that he still finds me attractive," Kat admitted. "That's all."

"Oh," Emma said. "For a moment I thought you were serious."

"I am serious," Kat said, her voice turning sharp. "But just not about remarrying Brent."

Emma felt her head beginning to pound. "Mother, I can not keep up with you."

Kat smiled. "Your father was poor when I met him, you know."

"I know."

"Like your young man," Kat continued.

Emma looked at her mother sharply. "But Daddy was never after your money!"

"I know that," Kat replied. "But he spent our entire marriage proving that to the world. He was never home, always off doing business, earning more and more millions to prove that he hadn't married me for *my* millions—"

"So you think that's what would happen if I marry Kurt, is that your point?" Emma asked.

Kat raised her eyebrows at her daughter. "Who says I have a point? We're just two girlfriends gabbing away at lunch!"

"Kurt isn't like that," Emma continued, ignoring her mother's comment. "He doesn't even care about money! I think he wishes I weren't rich!"

"You don't really believe that, do you?" Kat asked.

"I know him, you don't," Emma snapped.

"Oh, silly, let's not fight!" Kat said, reaching for Emma's hand. "Your father is better, and it's a beautiful day, and I'm feeling young and foolish! I'm sure everyone out here thinks we're sisters."

Emma sighed and stared out at the endless ocean. *I'm nothing like my silly, vain mother and Kurt is nothing like my workaholic father,* she vowed. *And we will not, not, not make the same mistakes!*

"So, your mother thinks we're going to turn out just like her and your father?" Kurt asked. "Have I got that right?"

Emma and Kurt were in Kurt's car that evening, driving back from the hospital to the island. Brent was resting comfortably in his private room and seemed much better. Kat was with him—Emma and Kurt had left them cozily watching TV together.

"Something like that," Emma said, leaning against Kurt's shoulder. "It's often difficult to follow my mother's train of thought."

Kurt stopped at a red light and leaned

over to kiss Emma. "Well, she knows nothing about us, does she?"

"Nothing," Emma agreed, happily returning his kiss. "What did you cook for dinner? I'm starved!"

Kurt had invited Emma over for dinner, promising to cook her something wonderful.

"Actually, we have a better chef than me on point tonight," Kurt said, turning onto his block. "My dad."

"Oh," Emma said. "I thought it was just going to be us."

"Well, I think it's time you and Dad got to know each other," Kurt said, pulling into his driveway. "Do you mind?"

"No, of course not," Emma assured Kurt. *Liar,* she thought. *I do, too, mind. After all the stress I've been through with Kat and Dad I want Kurt all to myself tonight.*

"C'mon in," Kurt said, leading her inside.

Emma followed Kurt into the modest home he shared with his sisters and his father. They went into the living room together, a room that Emma had rarely been in.

Sitting on the slightly threadbare couch was Kurt's father, Tom Ackerman. He was a handsome, weathered-looking man in his early forties, with eyes the same clear blue as his son's.

"Hi, Dad," Kurt said. "You remember Emma, right?"

"Hello, Emma," Mr. Ackerman said, rising to his full height of six feet one inch, and reaching out a work-hardened hand for Emma to shake.

Emma took his hand and shook it automatically, looking at Tom Ackerman. Except that his hair was a little thinner, his face more weathered, and he weighed about thirty more pounds more than Kurt, the resemblance between the two was unmistakable.

"Hello, Mr. Ackerman," Emma said, mustering all her politeness.

"Please," Kurt's father said, motioning to the brown easy chair near the couch, "sit down, Emma."

Emma sat down automatically. Kurt excused himself and went into the kitchen, saying that he was getting drinks for them all.

"My son has told me about your father, Emma. How are you holding up?" Mr. Ackerman asked her, leaning forward in his red flannel shirt and nondescript khaki work pants.

"Better, thank you," Emma said honestly, hoping that Kurt would return quickly from the kitchen and rescue her.

"That's a very difficult thing you've done," Mr. Ackerman said.

"Excuse me?" Emma asked, confused.

"Taking care of your father," Mr. Ackerman said. "Hard."

Emma nodded.

"But it sounds like you got everything right under control," Tom continued.

Do I hear admiration in his voice?

"Thank you, sir," Emma said. "It's a very good hospital he's in."

"No need to call me sir," Mr. Ackerman said, allowing a smile to come to his lips. "I work for a living." As he said these last words, he showed Emma his hard, callused, rugged hands.

"I . . . don't think calling you 'sir' has anything to do with whether or not you work for a living, Mr. Ackerman," Emma said, hoping she didn't sound like a total fool.

"That a fact," Kurt's father said, nodding slightly. "Has my boy helped you out any?"

"Kurt's helped me a lot," Emma replied honestly.

"Kurt tells me you were on your own at the hospital," Mr. Ackerman responded.

Where is Kurt anyway? I hope he's not leaving me alone here on purpose . . . oh, no, I bet his father put him up to this. He has something to say to me.

"That's not true," Emma said. "My mother came in."

"Humph," Mr. Ackerman said, making a sound deep in his throat. "My boy says you were still pretty much on your own."

"Well . . ." Emma began, ready to equivocate.

"Emma," Mr. Ackerman interrupted, "I'm a Mainer, and Mainers don't talk much. But I do have something I want to say to you. I know I've been hard on Kurt about you. I thought you were just another one of those pretty rich girls from off the island who couldn't tie their own shoelaces if their life depended on it."

Tom Ackerman looked directly into Emma's eyes. And she looked right back without flinching.

"My son told me I was wrong about you," Tom continued. "Well, what I've heard about your doings in the last week tells me he was right, and I was wrong. You stuck by your dad in his time of need and that's the most any child can do."

"Thank you," Emma said simply.

"You're welcome," Tom said, nodding briskly. "You're a fine young woman. That's what Kurt's momma was, too. A fine, fine woman."

Emma felt tears coming to her eyes. Maybe it was just everything she'd been through in the past week, or maybe it was exhaustion. But she hadn't realized how much Kurt's father's approval meant to her until just now, when she finally had it.

TWELVE

"So, I'm sure you understand why I'm leaving," Kat said, gingerly eyeing the cling peaches and cottage cheese plate that lay before her.

It was a whole week later, Kat and Emma were in the hospital cafeteria having lunch. Dr. Jones had just told them that Brent would definitely be released the following day—and Kat had just informed Emma that she was leaving.

"Mother," Emma said, taking a bite of her tuna salad and then putting down her fork. "The truth of the matter is, I will never understand you."

"Well, this board meeting of the New

York Arts Society is very important," Kat said. "I really do need to be there."

"Would you have gone if Daddy weren't being released?"

"Conjecture is a waste of time," Kat said, pushing the cottage cheese plate out of her way.

"But it seemed as if the two of you were getting to be . . ." Emma searched for the right word, "friends."

"Emma dear, let this be a lesson to you as you go through life—former lovers cannot be friends."

Former lovers. Kat and Daddy? Emma thought. *It's so hard to picture, but they had to have done it at least once—I mean, I exist. So if they're not friends, what are they?*

"—So, naturally Austin is very anxious for me to get back to New York," Kat concluded.

"Naturally," Emma repeated drily, even though she hadn't been listening to most of what Kat had said. "Mother, if you are so crazed for Austin, why did you come here and stay with Daddy all this time? I still don't understand."

"I've already explained that," Kat said

briskly, sipping her black coffee. "God, this is swill," she added, making a face at the coffee cup.

"Well, if you and Daddy aren't friends, what are you?"

"We'll see, won't we," Kat said coolly.

"You are driving me nuts, Mother," Emma said with exasperation. "What does that mean?"

"If you must know, I've invited your father to come and visit me when I go to the chalet in Switzerland next month," Kat said.

"You *what?*"

"Be a dear and don't mention this to Austin," Kat added.

"You invited Daddy to—"

"Yes," Kat interrupted Emma. She smiled slyly at her daughter. "I said former lovers couldn't be friends. I didn't say *current* lovers couldn't be friends."

Emma's mouth gaped open. "You mean you and Daddy—?"

"Of course not," Kat scoffed. "The man just had a heart attack. However, Dr. Jones tells me that next month Brent should be in divine shape."

"But, but . . . you hate each other," Emma sputtered.

Kat leaned forward toward her daughter. "Emma, no one ever made me feel as beautiful as your father. He still does."

Emma stared at her mother. "Are you two . . . getting back together?"

"Heavens, no!" Kat cried. "I would never remarry your father!"

"But you would . . . ?" Emma knew her mother would follow her implication.

"I might," Kat replied, a girlish twinkle in her eyes. "And don't bother looking so shocked, it doesn't become you. Oh, one other thing. Don't mention this to Princess, either."

Emma felt dizzy as her mother segued from one shocker into the next. "I doubt that I will ever speak to Princess again in my life," Emma replied, "and just how do you know about her, anyway?"

"She sent your father a letter from Florida, which was lying on his nightstand when he went to the bathroom," Kat explained. "This Princess person wrote that she was such a sensitive and delicate flower that she couldn't possibly face Brent's illness, and other such drivel—she dotted the 'i' in

Princess with a happy face, by the way—I may have read this urgent missive to your father," Kat concluded.

"Mother!"

"Oh, who cares, that little money-grubbing bimbo is out of the picture, anyway," Kat continued blithely.

Emma shook her head in amazement. "You are . . . unbelievable."

"Thank you!" Kat said with a gay smile. "Now, let's talk about you."

"That would be novel," Emma said dryly.

Kat let the dig pass. "Brent told me about your interest in monkeys."

"Primates, Mother," Emma corrected her. "Primates. Not monkeys."

"Whatever," Kat said. "Brent tells me you want to study them, though I can't imagine why."

"They interest me," Emma said defensively.

"You couldn't be interested in French literature or art history?" Kat asked. "You are so talented in those subjects."

Emma ignored her mother's question.

"Did Daddy tell you I'm thinking of transferring?" Emma asked.

"Indeed he did," Kat replied, "to some school somewhere in France."

"To Lyons," Emma said. "In France. To the University of Lyons."

"I have a passport," Kat said nonchalantly.

"What does *that* have to do with anything?" Emma asked, totally confused.

"I'll need it to visit you there," Kat replied. "Concorde to Paris, TGV train to Lyons—I can be there in six hours. Wonderful restaurants in Lyons."

Emma was speechless. She sat there staring at her mother. "I can't believe this. I've gone through hell trying to get up the nerve to tell you I wanted to change my life, and you're saying—"

"I'm saying you should study wherever and whatever you want," Kat said simply. She ran her hand through her perfectly streaked blond hair. "Go to France. God knows it's cultured enough! I admit I'd rather have you go to France to study French, but it's your life, darling."

Emma looked suspiciously at her mother. "What am I missing here? You've dictated every moment of my life, always concerned about how things look and if I'm with the 'right' people . . . and now you're blithely telling me to—"

"Emma, you are too young to tie yourself down," Kat said earnestly, leaning close to Emma. "France will be an adventure for you, with—as you just pointed out—the 'right' people. I'll give you names and numbers."

And then it dawned on Emma. "This is about Kurt, isn't it!"

Kat feigned a look of innocence. "You asked for my approval to go study in France and I'm giving it—!"

"You don't want me to marry Kurt, and you think if I go to France in the fall it will be the end of our relationship!"

"Well, that's a distinct possibility, isn't it?" Kat asked smugly. "Or is he planning to drive a taxi in France?"

"Nothing is going to come between Kurt and me," Emma stated, grabbing the edge of the table. "Nothing!"

"Well, good," Kat replied. "Then I guess your going to Europe for an extended period of time will be the proof of just how right you are." Kat grabbed her purse and scarf and stood up. "Come with me while I say good-bye to your father."

Emma got up silently, trying to figure out how she could have won and lost at the exact same time.

At ten o'clock that night, the Play Café on Sunset Island was packed. Emma, Carrie, and Sam had arrived about a half-hour earlier and managed to find themselves a booth near the pool table and order a large pizza with everything. Sam was going on about some guy she'd met on the beach, and Emma smiled at her two best friends. Sam had on a sheer, oversize print dress from the Salvation Army with a black bodysuit underneath it, and, of course, her cowboy boots. Carrie had on a red rugby shirt, jeans, and a backwards baseball cap. A feeling of happiness came over Emma—that her dad was okay, that she was back with her friends, that life really could go back to normal.

"So, how do you feel about your mom leaving?" Carrie asked Emma, when Sam finished her rambling story.

"Mixed." Emma shrugged. "I actually talked to her about going to study in France in the fall." Emma told them the entire conversation with her mother.

"So, the deal is, she's telling you to go because she thinks you'll break up with Kurt?" Sam asked, reaching for another slice of pizza.

"Right," Emma agreed.

"Huh, quel-diabolical," Sam opined.

"Is she right?" Carrie asked pointedly.

"No! Of course not!" Emma cried. "Kurt's worried about the same thing—that's why he's pushing for us to make some kind of commitment. But I believe that if it's meant to be, it'll be—nothing is going to change what I feel for him!"

"But you'd be surrounded by French guys!" Sam exclaimed. "Dark, brooding artsy types with that sexy accent—"

"I love Kurt," Emma said simply.

"But are you ready to be engaged-to-be-engaged?" Carrie asked.

"I don't know," Emma said honestly. "I mean, I'm ready to make a commitment to Kurt—I already have—but I don't see why it has to be . . . I don't know . . . defined."

"Kurt's gonna say if you really love him, you'll do it," Sam guessed, wiping some tomato sauce off her mouth. "Not that I think that's a good reason to do it, by the way."

"It's not," Emma agreed, idly stirring her iced-tea with a straw. "I don't want to be pressured by Kurt or my mother or any-one!"

"Good for you," Carrie approved.

"I guess I'll have to wait and discuss it with Kurt," Emma said with a shrug.

"He's a great guy," Carrie said. "I mean, look at all the time he spent with you at the hospital visiting your dad."

"My father likes Kurt," Emma said with a fond smile. "Kurt reminds me of my father, actually . . ."

"Both poor guys who fell for rich girls?" Sam asked.

"But Kurt would never become a worka-holic like my dad," Emma said. "That's one way in which they are totally different."

Carrie and Sam stared at her.

"Well, they are!" Emma exclaimed defen-sively.

"Kurt works two jobs, he never has any free time—" Sam began.

"Sam, he's putting himself through col-lege!" Emma protested.

"Is Kurt going with you to pick up your dad from the hospital tomorrow?" Carrie asked, expertly changing the subject.

"Yes," Emma said, still feeling disgruntled about Sam's remark. "Notice how Kurt has enough time to come with me!"

"Okay, you're right, I apologize," Sam said. "You know I think Kurt is a great guy and a total babe."

"Thanks," Emma said.

"But I still think you ought to consider those French kisses when you're—"

"So are you putting your dad right on a plane for Florida?" Carrie interrupted.

"Actually, Kurt and I are planning to take him to the golf club," Emma replied.

"Girlfriend, I think you have finally gone over the top," Sam decided, finishing the last of the pizza. "Your dad is not ready to play golf."

"I know," Emma agreed. "But we're still going to take him there."

"Why? You want to return to the scene of the crime?" Carrie asked.

"Something like that," Emma replied, smiling enigmatically. "There's something important that my dad needs to do before he goes home."

"Are we supposed to guess?" Sam asked, slightly miffed.

"No," Emma said. "You're supposed to

wait until tomorrow night, when I tell you."

"You know I hate secrets unless I'm in on them," Sam said.

"I know," Emma said, "but just this once . . . suffer!"

THIRTEEN

Emma looked over at her father, who was standing near the guard railing of the Sunset Island ferry. Emma had picked him up at Maine Medical Center an hour before, and after getting a lecture from Dr. Jones about how lucky Brent was to be alive, they were heading back to Sunset Island—the Hewitts' car was on the transport deck directly below them.

"Emma," Brent said, looking out at the wheeling terns that were flying escort with the ferry as it slowly made its way across Casco Bay from the mainland to Sunset Island. "Here's my cliché for the day: it's good to be alive."

Emma smiled and put her hand over her father's. *If you didn't know,* Emma thought, *you'd never be able to tell that this man just had a major heart attack. He looks exactly the same as he did when he showed up on the island—he's a bit thinner, that's all. He's even wearing the same awful outfit as the he was on the day he collapsed!*

"It's good to have you alive, Dad," Emma said simply.

"See those birds there?" Brent pointed to the terns. "I remember thinking that I would never see a bird again." He stared out at the terns making lazy circles in the sky. "I talked with your mother about your studying in France, you know," Brent said.

"She told me."

"So I guess you know it's okay with her," Emma's father said, looking at his daughter.

"Dad, it's not because I have her blessing," Emma said with a sigh, "it's because she believes if I go I'll end up breaking up with Kurt. She considers France the lesser of two evils."

Brent Cresswell looked at his daughter. "You love this boy?"

"Yes, I do," Emma said.

"Then don't let anything come between you," Brent said. "Love is too hard to come by in this world. And in the end, it's the only thing that matters a damn, anyway."

"I'll try to remember that, Daddy," Emma said softly.

Emma could see the Sunset Island ferry-port clearly now as the ferry approached it. Standing on the dock was a familiar figure in jeans and a T-shirt, his brown, sun-streaked hair ruffling in the breeze. And although Emma was too far away to make out his features, it didn't matter. She knew every one by heart.

Kurt. I love you.

"Dad, we need to make a quick stop before we go to the Inches's to pick up your stuff," Emma said when the three of them were heading away from the ferry.

"The beach for a little tackle football?" Brent quipped.

"I'd say you're still a week away from that, sir," Kurt said with a laugh.

"Actually, we need to stop by the golf club to pick up your clubs," Emma said, expertly maneuvering the BMW around a curve. "The pro called me about them."

"That's right," her dad said to her, "I forgot all about them."

Emma drove directly to the country club, and pulled into the special lot near the golf course. The three of them walked into the club lounge.

There, two men were sitting on a couch and a chair near one another, with a tray in front of them. On the tray was a bottle of champagne and a bottle of nonalcoholic sparkling cider. The two men stood up as the threesome approached them.

"Dad," Emma said, her eyes glistening slightly, "I'd like to introduce you to two friends of yours."

Emma could see her father smiling politely, but in his eyes she could tell that he thought he didn't know these men at all.

"This is Peter Harrison," Emma said, indicating the shorter of the two men, "and this is William Fishbine." The two men smiled broadly and stuck their hands out to Emma's father.

Emma looked at her father as he shook hands with the two men. A flash of recognition came across Brent Cresswell's face.

"These are the men who saved your

life," Emma said quietly to her father.

"I don't know how I can ever thank you," Brent Cresswell said, his voice choked with emotion.

Peter Harrison laughed. "You're doing fine," he said, "just being here. Anyway, all I did was make a call. Willie was the one who did the real work!"

"And how," William Fishbine said. "We can't wait till we can play golf with you!"

Emma looked at the two men and grinned. A few days earlier Kurt had suggested that Emma call the people who had saved her father's life and arrange for them all to meet.

Kurt put his arm around Emma. "This is my boyfriend, Kurt Ackerman," Emma said proudly. "This was all his idea."

Brent Cresswell looked at Kurt, trying hard to control his emotions. "Thank you, son," he said softly.

They all sat down, and Kurt poured the drinks into the waiting glasses as Emma watched, lost in thought. *Daddy called Kurt "son". And I liked it! Maybe I am ready to make the commitment Kurt wants. Maybe I really am . . .*

"Hey, is this juice supposed to be for me?" Brent protested.

"Dr. Jones said no alcohol," Emma reminded her father.

"Hey, I'm an A.A. man, myself," Peter Harrison said, "I'll stick to the juice, too."

Look at Peter Harrison, Emma thought. *Short, balding, kind of fat—you'd never think he would be a life saver. Look at William Fishbine—tall, skinny, glasses, kind of a big nose, a funny birthmark on his neck—is this the guy I'd think would be a hero? But if Fishbine hadn't known CPR, and if Harrison hadn't had a mobile phone in his golf cart, my father might not be here now. He might be dead.*

"I want to propose a toast," Emma said, reaching down and picking up one of the glasses full of champagne. "This toast is to two heroes," Emma said simply, "two men to whom I'll be grateful forever."

They all clinked glasses and drank.

Emma looked over at her father. He was smiling broadly, but tears were rolling down his cheeks.

Then she looked at the other two men. They were crying a bit, too.

It was only then that Emma saw one

of her own tears fall into her champagne glass.

What the heck, she thought.

She raised the glass to her mouth and drained it.

Emma walked along the main beach next to Kurt, hand-in-hand, as the sun slowly began to set in the far distance. After spending some time at the club Emma and Kurt had taken Brent Cresswell to the Inches's house to pick up his stuff, and then had driven him to the airport.

"What are you thinking?" Kurt asked her. "You're so quiet."

"I'm thinking that I'm incredibly lucky," Emma said softly. She turned to face him. "And that I love you very much."

"Gee, I was thinking the same thing," Kurt said with a grin, putting his arms around Emma's waist.

"You know, I once read that it's in times of crisis that you can tell who your real friends are," Emma mused. "I guess one good thing that came out of all this is I found out just how many great friends I really have."

"Well, at the risk of turning you into a

giant, walking ego, you're pretty special," Kurt told her, brushing some hair out of her eyes.

Emma stared earnestly into Kurt's eyes. "Kurt, I really think I'm going to go to France in the fall."

Kurt's face fell.

"Don't you see?" she pressed. "I can't give up what I really want to do out of . . . of fear that we'll lose each other!" Emma explained.

"But what if we do?" Kurt whispered.

"Don't you know how much I love you?" Emma said earnestly. "Distance can't change that! It *won't* change that!"

"But how can you be sure?" Kurt asked.

"I can't," Emma admitted, tears coming to her eyes. "But after what happened with my father it's like . . . like I see now that we really don't have forever to live out our dreams. And, Kurt, this is my dream!"

"Oh, Emma—"

"But you're my dream, too," Emma continued. "I'd be a fool to lose you—and as Kat Cresswell says, 'There are no fools in the Cresswell family.' "

Kurt tried to smile at her, but his eyes were filled with sadness.

"Kurt, you're the very best thing that ever happened to me in my life."

Kurt stared out at the ocean, then looked back at Emma. "I don't want to hold you back, Em. I guess we'll just have to . . . take it as it comes."

"I love you, Kurt," Emma whispered. "I could never love anyone the way I love you."

With the waves crashing on the shore, and the gulls calling to each other in the sky, Emma kissed Kurt with all of her heart, hoping he would understand.

And from the way he kissed her back, Emma knew, at last, that he did.

Dear Readers,

I have been traveling so much lately that it's a pleasure to be back home for a couple of weeks. As always, I've been getting the most incredible, awesome, fabulous letters from you.

Listen, a lot of you are still worried that I'm going to stop writing books about Emma, Sam, and Carrie just because there is a spin-off about Darcy and Molly. I mean, I've gotten hundreds of letters pleading with me for more Sunset books about our dynamic trio. So, to Carrie Wayne of West Pittson, Pennsylvania, and Kimberly Provost of Louisville, Kentucky, and Samantha Star Raines (great name, by the way) of Iola, Kansas, and all the rest of you out there, THERE ARE MANY MORE BOOKS COMING ABOUT EMMA, SAM, AND CARRIE. I PROMISE! I hope you enjoy the books about Darcy and Molly, too. Now there are two series about fantastic, romantic Sunset Island!

Some special messages to some special fans: to Jessika White who lives on an air force base somewhere—I can't read your return address, so I can't write back to you. Thank you so much for the wonderful present! To Jessica Hernandez from Bakersfield, California—your letter was just great, but you forgot to give me a return address! And to the mysterious S.S. from Escondido, California—what exactly does S.S. stand for? Secret Service? Sunset Scandal?

SUNSET ISLAND MAILBOX

Dear Cherie,

I am writing because I wanted to tell you how much I enjoy reading your Sunset Island books. They are different from every other series. I was curious to find out what you think about books being taken out of schools and libraries because they are "inappropriate." Do you think this is unfair?

Sincerely,
Angie Chan
Irvine, California

Dear Angie,

It troubles me a lot when I read about books being banned from certain schools or libraries. Censorship is a dangerous thing. I'd love to hear from you out there on this issue. Have any of you had books banned from your school or library? How did you handle it?

Best,
Cherie

Dear Cherie,
I just wanted to tell you that you are my all-time favorite author. I was just wondering if you have ever had three special friends like Carrie, Emma and Sam?

Love,
Misty Hefner
Statesville, North Carolina

Dear Misty,

My very best friends when I was growing up were Judy Harris and Ina Strichartz. We were inseparable. Judy and I used to charge kids in our neighborhood a quarter apiece for ballet lessons—even though we'd never had a ballet lesson in our lives! Now, that's nerve! Sounds like something Sam would do, doesn't it?

Best,
Cherie

Dear Cherie,

The Sunset Island books are the best books I've ever read, and believe me, I've read a lot of books. I have a friend who reminds me a lot of Darcy. I also know some people just like Diana, but I won't mention any names, because everyone I know reads Sunset Island. Who did you base Darcy on?

Your #1 fan,
Stephanie East
Ada, Ohio

Dear Stephanie,

Don't we all know someone sort of like Diana, who just loves to make other people miserable? How do they even face themselves in the mirror, that's what I'd like to know! I based Darcy on my sister-in-law, Judy, who is the coolest thing walking. I wanted to create a heroine who isn't model-thin, who is smart, assertive and can take care of herself. The E.S.P. part just seemed like it would be fun to write about! Can you imagine how cool it would be to know the future? Or would it be incredibly scary? What do you think?

Best,
Cherie

GOT A TERRIFIC IDEA FOR A SUNSET ISLAND STORY? MAIL IT IN! IF YOUR STORY IDEA IS THE WINNER, CHERIE BENNETT WILL TURN IT INTO AN ACTUAL BOOK–AND YOU WILL WIN A FREE TRIP TO MEET HER IN NASHVILLE, TENNESSEE! 100 RUNNERS-UP WILL RECEIVE A SUNSET ISLAND T-SHIRT!

No purchase necessary. See below for complete details.

SUNSET ISLAND™ SUMMER '93 CONTEST RULES

GRAND PRIZE: Grand Prize winner's story idea will be the basis of a future Sunset Island novel. Round-trip transportation for Grand Prize winner and one legal guardian to Nashville, Tennesee; a two-night stay at a hotel, including all meals (but not including personal expenses, i.e. laundry, telephone calls); dinner with Cherie Bennett, author of the SUNSET ISLAND novels published by The Berkley Publishing Group.

100 RUNNERS-UP: A Sunset Island T-shirt

NO PURCHASE NECESSARY.

1. All entries must be clearly printed or typewritten. On the upper left-hand corner of an 8½" x 11" sheet of paper, put your name, address, telephone number, and date of birth. On the same piece of paper, in your own words, typewritten, or clearly printed, in one hundred words or less, write your own original plot idea, centering around any one or all three of these Sunset Island characters: Emma, Sam, and/or Carrie.
2. Entry must be postmarked no later than September 30, 1993. Not responsible for lost or misdirected mail. The winner and runners-up will be announced and notified by mail by January 15, 1994.
3. Entrant must be 17 years of age or younger. One entry per person. Entry is property of General Licensing Company, Inc. and will not be returned. The grand prize is the sole compensation for the winning entry. No substitution of prizes is permitted. Travel must be completed by August 31, 1994. Travel and accommodation dates subject to availability.
4. This contest is open to all residents of the continental U.S. seventeen years of age and younger. Void where prohibited by law. Employees and their families of The Putnam Berkley Group, MCA, Matsushita Electrical & Industrial Corporation, General Licensing Company, Inc., their respective affiliates, retailers, distributors, advertising, promotion, and production agencies are not eligible.
5. Taxes on all prizes are the sole responsibility of the prize-winner whose legal guardian may be required to sign and return a statement of eligibility within fourteen days of notification. Winner must assign all rights in the plot to General Licensing Company, Inc. The names and likenesses of the winner and the guardian may be used for promotional purposes.
6. In the event there are an insufficient number of entries that meet the minimum requirements of the judge, the sponsor reserves the right not to award all prizes.
7. Mail entries to: SUNSET ISLAND CONTEST
c/o General Licensing Company, Inc.
24 West 25th Street
New York, NY 10010
8. For the name of the grand prize winner, send a stamped, self-addressed envelope to SUNSET ISLAND CONTEST WINNER, c/o General Licensing Company, Inc., 24 West 25th Street, New York, NY 10010